To Truly
See

Kristin Billerbeck

Heartsong Presents

To my wonderful husband (a true Prince Charming) and my
grandmother for their continuing encouragement.

A note from the author:
*I love to hear from my readers! You may correspond with me
by writing:* **Kristin Billerbeck**
Author Relations
PO Box 719
Uhrichsville, OH 44683

ISBN 1-57748-425-8

TO TRULY SEE

Cover illustration by Kay Salem

PRINTED IN THE U.S.A.

one

Brenda Turner stood in the empty examining room, buttoned her pale green silk blouse, and tucked it into her straight ivory skirt. Slipping her feet into her sling-back heels, she sat to await the doctor's return. A familiar muffled ringing sounded from the brushed leather briefcase at her feet. She reached for the tiny cellular phone, grabbing her hairbrush at the same time.

She pressed a small button on the phone. "Brenda Turner." After listening for a moment, she impatiently interrupted. "Tell the printer, they *must* be finished by Thursday. If I don't have those brochures in my hand *on time,* Atlas Printing will be a memory. I'll make sure of that."

She listened for a few seconds before interrupting again. "Take charge, Katie! They may conveniently forget that Star Digital is their most valuable client, but it's your job to remind them! Look, Katie, my appointment is here, I'll see you in the office soon." Brenda folded the small telephone quickly and slammed it into her briefcase. Frustrated, she wondered whether she would ever find an administrative assistant who could handle the pressure. She tossed her blond hair and looked intently at the doctor as he entered, her work momentarily forgotten.

A short, stocky man in a white lab coat, Dr. Wilhelm wore a solemn face and carried an oversized file envelope filled with x-rays. "Miss Turner, these are the results of your latest MRI. . .and these are the results of your first one two years ago." He clipped the two negatives on a lighted board and Brenda's brain loomed brightly before her. She walked toward the pictures, fascinated by the images.

"Wow, look at those wrinkles. . .she must have an incredible IQ," Brenda joked, trying to make light of the situation.

Dr. Wilhelm smiled thinly and proceeded with his clinical diagnosis, but he avoided looking his patient in the eye. "Miss Turner, these white spots on your brain here represent what we call placquing, indicative of demyelination. Your double vision, loss of balance, and dizzy spells are the result of a demyelinating disease."

Brenda looked at the doctor inquisitively. His ridiculous double-talk irritated her. Noting her angry confusion, the doctor continued, "Your central nervous system is made up of many wires insulated with a material called myelin, just like real wire would be insulated with a rubber coating. Something is attacking your myelin, replacing it with scar tissue. Judging from your symptoms, I'd say this is a brain stem attack, which is sending strange messages to your eyes and ears, affecting your equilibrium."

"Look, Dr. Wilhelm, I'm a bright woman, but you're not speaking English. In laymen's terms, please, do I have a brain tumor or what?" Brenda stepped closer to the doctor, using her 5' 10" stature to try to intimidate him.

"Miss Turner, I am diagnosing you with multiple sclerosis." The blunt response hit Brenda like a freight train. Her shoulders dropped as her breath left her. She looked pleadingly at the doctor for a smile, anxious to share in the joke, but his face remained grave. She found the chair behind her with her hands and slowly sat down, trying to absorb the information. The young executive had been taught to keep her cool amidst troubling news, but this had thrown her.

She remained seated and spoke after regaining her composure. "Meaning?"

"Myelin can repair itself and it already has once before. You see your old films show these white spots." The doctor pointed to two small white blurs. "But in the latest MRI, the old spots are gone. What you have is very likely relapsing-remitting MS, which means you may fully recover from the symptoms you're experiencing. . .just like you did last time. There is the possibility you may not, although my guess would be that it would continue on a remitting course for quite some time." The doctor finally looked her in the eye.

"Doctor, I can barely stand up with this dizziness. People at work are beginning to think I had one too many at lunch. How can I possibly work like this? There must be a pill or something—you know, to speed things up."

"Miss Turner, there are lots of medications to help minimize your symptoms, even a few that may slow the progression of the disease, but there is no cure for multiple sclerosis."

Brenda fumed at the negative answer. She couldn't abide by such powerlessness. Somebody had to have a better answer and she was determined to find it. She began roughly pulling the film down off the lighted screen.

"Very well, Dr. Wilhelm, I can see I'm going to need a second opinion on such a serious diagnosis. Thank you." Brenda's mind was racing, anxious to find the neurologist who would tell her what she wanted to hear. She placed the negatives under her arm and walked decisively from the room, slamming the door behind her.

The doctor craned his head cautiously around the corner and called tentatively after her. "Miss Turner, those MRI results belong to the hospital."

"It's my brain, I'd say they belong to me. My insurance paid for them, correct?" Turning quickly to storm away once again, Brenda stumbled and careened into the wall. She reached desperately for support and managed to salvage her balance, if not her dignity. She exited using the wall as her guide. The stout doctor shook his head sorrowfully and returned to his office.

৵

Brenda turned up the volume on her surround-sound stereo while a motivational speaker preached the art of negotiation. No matter how loud she turned the tape, Dr. Wilhelm's vicious words echoed louder: *multiple sclerosis*.

Her shiny, black BMW convertible drove as if on autopilot, delivering Brenda to her office. She hastily squealed the sports car into her reserved parking space and collected the x-rays from the passenger seat. She folded them once carefully, hiding them in the large side pocket of her briefcase. Worried that she might lose her balance again, she removed her taupe heels and replaced them with bright white running shoes.

Brenda eagerly approached the mirrored-glass high-rise that felt like home. She pressed her name badge to the electronic security panel and the door clicked for her entry. The familiar steel gray lobby felt like a warm arm around her.

Katie Cummings, Brenda's secretary, rushed past the rows of cubicles, frantically waving her arms, "Brenda, you're here. The VP of engineering has been looking for you all morning. Are you ready with the campaign? He says hardware has completed the prototype today and software will be ready by the weekend. He's been screaming 'where is marketing?' for an hour. You turned your cell phone off." Katie's face was anguished and when Brenda didn't speak, she continued. "Brenda, I wish you would delegate more authority. Your staff has been yelling at me all morning. I'm not a punching bag."

"Katie, I'm sorry you had trouble, but how often am I ever out of the office?" The tall blond sat calmly behind her large mahogany desk and allowed her eyes to wander confidently over the sketches and copy changes in front of her. Brenda knew she would meet the impossible deadline, she always did. That's how she had become vice president of marketing at only twenty-seven. Her secret was time; she devoted all of it to work. Outside her door she watched middle-aged engineers banging on their keyboards, stuck in their tiny cubicles while she sat comfortably in her spacious office overlooking the man-made lakes and waterfalls outside the building. A corner of her mouth lifted smugly as she recalled her accomplishments.

"Katie, tell engineering and software to worry about engineering and software; the marketing's ready to go—as always." Katie smiled and strode assuredly toward the engineering department, "Oh, and Katie, before you go, I'm doing a little research project. Would you please find me the best neurologist in town? And I'm having dinner with someone from Cyreck, his name's on my calendar. Find out about him."

"Absolutely," Katie made mental notes and left.

Brenda's head was spinning. She tried to read a report, but her eyes would not focus. The lines jumped from on the page like a v-hold on a television set gone berserk. She closed her eyes and opened them again, but the results were the same. She clamored in her purse for a mirror and looked at her reflection. She closed one eye, concentrating on the bright blue of the other. It didn't appear to be moving, but the sights in front of her continued to jump. She closed her left eye and peered at the right. It also remained motionless while the mirror appeared to leap relentlessly. *What is going on?*

Instantly, Brenda recalled the doctor's ugly words. *It can't be multiple sclerosis,* she thought, *that's when people can't walk. My legs feel fine. I just feel so tired and dizzy. Why today, when I have so much to do?* She rubbed the back of her neck and kicked off her bulky athletic shoes underneath the desk. *Caffeine. Of course! I haven't had any coffee today.*

Brenda leaned across her desk and buzzed Katie on the intercom. "Katie, would you mind ordering me a mocha and making it a double shot? I'm just falling asleep today and I can't explain it."

"Perhaps if you went home once in a while and used that device called a bed, you might feel more awake," Katie said sarcastically.

Brenda had grown very dependent upon her new assistant since she had started six months earlier. Although Katie was younger, she acted with a wisdom that Brenda failed to understand. "Katie, your poor husband, do you nag him to death too?"

"Nope, he knows the way home. Besides, you're much easier to irritate." Katie said the words sweetly and Brenda knew she was sincere. Katie leaned against the door frame. "Seriously, Brenda, I worry about you. I've never seen you eat a meal that didn't involve a sales pitch or leave early to do something fun. . .and meeting your physical trainer upstairs in the gym doesn't count!"

As usual, the slender young executive ignored the prodding from her secretary. "Just get the mocha, please." Brenda picked up the phone to return her calls. She had tried to answer her e-mail and finish her reports, but her eyes simply wouldn't focus; they seemed to be getting worse. She knew she would have to delegate some things if she was going to make the deadline. Failure was not an option.

&a.

"Brenda, here's your double mocha. I added whipped cream today, maybe we'll put a little meat on your bones. I took the liberty of arranging an appointment with Dr. Luke Marcusson, noted neurologist, researcher, and neurosurgeon at Stanford." Katie deepened her voice to sound impressive. "He can see you next month." Katie brought in the coffee, iced, as her boss preferred, and watched as Brenda scooped the white topping off the drink and into the garbage below. Katie just shook her head, expecting it.

"Next month? No, Katie, I can't wait until next month. I need this research as soon as possible. Never mind. Just get me his number." Anticipating the request, Katie stepped forward and handed her the number.

"Brenda?" Katie dropped her voice to above a whisper.

"What is it, Katie?" Brenda glanced up impatiently.

"Your blouse is misbuttoned," Katie whispered discreetly, closing the door behind her as she exited.

Brenda rolled her eyes, disgusted by her carelessness. She strained to focus on the number in front of her. She fumbled with the buttons on her blouse and screamed at the door in frustration, "*Katie!*"

The secretary's face was white when she opened the door, "What is it?"

"Get this quack on the phone. My phone's not working," Brenda barked. *How can I possibly work with everything jumping like this?*

Katie's soothing voice came over the intercom, "Dr. Marcusson's nurse is on the phone. Brenda, be nice. Not everyone understands you the way I do."

Brenda picked up the phone, "Who am I speaking to?"

"This is LeAnne, Dr. Marcusson's nurse. Dr. Marcusson is

booked for new patients until next month. Can I help you?"

"Are you a neurologist?"

"No, I'm Dr. Marcusson's nurse."

"Then you can't help me. I want to talk to the doctor. Tell him it's his sister Brenda." Elevator music floated through the phone and Brenda tapped her foot impatiently during the wait.

A rich, deep voice came over the line, "Since I have no sisters, I'm going to assume you have something important to tell me." Brenda could sense the smile in his voice and was suddenly embarrassed by her forwardness.

"I'm sorry, Dr. Marcusson. Dr. Wilhelm diagnosed me with multiple sclerosis today. I'm anxious for a second opinion and I understand you're quite renowned."

"Dr. Wilhelm's a very competent neurologist. Nevertheless, I understand your need for a second opinion with such a serious diagnosis. Why don't you tell me a little about your symptoms?"

"Well, my head feels as though it's buzzing, like I'm slightly tipsy with alcohol. My eyes won't focus, everything appears to be jumping and I'm seeing double when I look to the left. My hands and feet are always freezing, while the rest of me is hot and I'm inexplicably exhausted."

"I'll tell you what, since you are 'family,' " he paused to let her hear the chastisement, "if you can meet me in my office at 6:30, I'll go over your MRI results with you. I assume you managed to get a copy of your films." Once again, Brenda flushed with embarrassment. Apparently, Dr. Marcusson had a full understanding of her boldness.

"Six-thirty. . .? Uh, I have an appoint—no, I'll be there," Brenda knew she couldn't turn down the appointment when she had been so brash. Dr. Marcusson seemed to have a sense of humor, but Brenda didn't want to push it.

"I have surgery scheduled for this afternoon, so if I'm a few minutes late, relax for a few minutes and *don't* read a magazine. Give your eyes a rest. And bring a list of questions you may have. I'll put my nurse on the line and you can give her your phone number just in case."

"Thank you, Doctor." Brenda spoke sweetly to the nurse, trying to make up for her earlier rudeness. LeAnne wasn't appeased and gave Brenda a slice of her own coldness. After the phone call, Brenda packed up her briefcase with reports. She agonized over how long it had taken her to get the appointment with Cyreck, but knew she wouldn't be of any use this evening, anyway. Brenda delegated the meeting to one of her product managers, then made a beeline for Katie with final instructions.

Katie's cubicle was always filled with flowers, thank you cards and smiling photos that looked like ads for diversity training. Brenda often wondered how anyone had time for so many friends, but chalked it up to the petite brunette's constant cheerfulness and bubbly personality. *People are just attracted to women like her.* She was talking on the phone, intermittently typing on the keyboard of one computer and navigating the mouse on another. When she saw Brenda in her cubicle, she lifted a short forefinger to tell her boss she'd only be a second and quickly hung up.

Katie addressed Brenda, "Your dinner meeting—"

"Don't worry about it, Mike's going to handle it. It's his problem now. I'm going home for the afternoon. If you need me, just call."

"Brenda, are you all right?" Katie looked deeply concerned.

"I'm fine, just fighting a little flu bug, I think." Brenda balanced herself against Katie's gray laminate desk and pretended to trip over a shoelace, to hide her balance woes.

"Well, I'll say a prayer for you tonight," Katie stated easily.

Brenda threw Katie a condescending grin. She thought her secretary's naiveté and penchant for prayer was sweet.

two

Brenda spent the afternoon in a deep sleep. She awoke with just enough time to make it to her appointment. Amazingly refreshed after her nap, she noted that her eyes and balance were nearly normal. She rushed down the front steps to her BMW and raced to Stanford University Hospital. Her appointment was in one of the small buildings next to the main hospital.

Dr. Marcusson's office was elegantly decorated and smelled of new carpet. Burgundy wing-back chairs filled the corners of the waiting room and a long, supple leather sofa was placed between them. The walls were finished with a gray marbled wallpaper and a single, colorful painting hung over the sofa. On the coffee table were the latest issues of *People, Newsweek,* and *Reader's Digest*. Brenda's eyes were drawn to a large plaque that stated, "I can do all things through Christ who strengthens me." Immediately she wanted to flee. "Katie!" She clicked her tongue. "I should have known she'd find me some religious doctor."

Katie had repeatedly invited Brenda to church. Right now it seemed like her secretary's search for the best neurologist went as far as a Sunday social. *He's affiliated with Stanford Hospital, so he must be qualified.* Brenda searched the office until her eyes lit upon a diploma. *Stanford University Medical School.* Brenda was encouraged to know that Dr. Marcusson had indeed been educated at the world-renowned school.

"Brenda Turner?" It was the deep-toned voice Brenda remembered from the phone. Feeling guilty for seeking clues to his credentials, Brenda jumped slightly. She turned to extend her hand and was completely taken aback.

Dr. Luke Marcusson stood well over six feet and for once, at 5' 10", Brenda felt petite, even in heels. His light brown hair was parted to the left and shaped in a short, conservative style.

His eyes appeared to be brown, but under the receding lights they showed a hint of green. A warm smile crossed his face and Brenda thought she'd faint at the sight of it, leaving her uncharacteristically speechless. He was casually dressed in a pair of khakis and a forest green golf shirt that wrapped loosely around his wide, muscular shoulders.

Brenda was overwhelmed that a man's mere presence could render her silent. Her next thought was to keep her medical issues quiet, especially after noting that his left hand was free of a wedding ring. *He looks more like a fireman than a physician!*

Brenda stumbled as she tried to recover herself, "Yes. . .Dr. Marcusson, I assume." She reached out and lost control of the oversized negatives in her arms. The slippery film tumbled clumsily onto the gray tweed carpeting. Brenda's face flushed red and she bent over quickly to pick them up, knocking heads with the already kneeling doctor. She fell to the floor and closed her eyes in despair.

Dr. Marcusson held out his hand, apologized, and lifted her gently to her feet. He led her to the sofa before returning to gather the MRI results. He arranged the negatives in order and held one up to the light to study it.

"Miss Turner, your MRI shows a great deal of placquing. Much more than normal, especially around the brain stem area. With what I know of your symptoms and after seeing these negs, I'm afraid I would have to agree with Dr. Wilhelm. This definitely appears to be multiple sclerosis. We look for either multiple symptoms or multiple occurrences. In your case, each MRI shows both, making a diagnosis fairly straightforward. I'm sorry." He handed her back the film images, but she refused to take them as if they were the disease itself.

"But I walk fine—well, except for my balance. And I don't feel like this all the time. Most days I jog three miles on the treadmill." Brenda unconsciously smoothed her hands along her hips.

"There are no shortage of symptoms for MS, Miss Turner. And there are no two cases alike. There's the possibility that you will completely recover tomorrow, without treatment, and never see these symptoms again. There's also the small possibility that your symptoms could worsen. Relapsing-remitting MS is usually marked by full recoveries, such as you've had. If the course changes to worsening gradually, that is what we call chronic-progressive MS. Everything here points to relapsing-remitting disease, which is good news. I can't make you any promises, but there are a great deal of new treatments available. Seventy-five percent of all patients will never even need a wheelchair."

"A wheelchair?" Brenda was incensed, "Look, Dr. Marcusson, I am a very busy woman. I put myself through college, made it to vice president of marketing at Star Digital. I own my own home in Palo Alto. I don't have time to be sick, I'm on a deadline! So, what can I take?"

"Miss Turner, this disease doesn't care about your credentials. Your best defense is to take some time off and sleep this flare-up away."

"Sleep? You mean during the day?" She looked up at him in disbelief.

"I mean whenever you can. You must reduce the stress in your life. I imagine your job can be stressful, but a little time off might do you well."

&

Luke ached for the beautiful young woman before him. He had diagnosed MS in many young patients and it was always difficult, but it had never before affected him in such a personal way. Her large, blue eyes gazed up at him, pleading for a report he was unable to offer. There was something different about the confidence she placed in his ability to immediately heal her. Her apparent faith forced him to take a certain responsibility he didn't want, but couldn't forfeit.

He rationalized that his deeper feelings probably stemmed from her being alone. To receive a serious diagnosis was trying, but to do it without support nearby seemed utterly devastating to him. He longed to pull her close and tell her that God loved her, and that with Him she would be fine, but he kept a professional distance.

He tried to avoid noticing her long, shapely legs and the toned body that appeared gym-earned, but for the first time in his career, his physician's eyes failed him. This woman had clearly affected him. His cousin Katie had told him of Brenda's harsh personality and he found himself mystified. Knowing she wasn't a Christian, Luke tried to shake the tempting feelings that stirred within him and forced his mind back to her medical condition.

"What are my options? Drugs? Vitamins? A vacation is not possible." Luke noticed how Brenda approached the subject without emotion, as though she were dealing with someone else's illness.

"Well, I would need to review your history and symptoms, but most likely we'd give you steroids to reduce the inflammation that's causing your symptoms."

"Steroids? Am I going to look like Arnold Schwarzenegger?"

"No, I'm afraid these steroids turn muscle into fat." Luke went over a list of symptoms with her and stopped mid-sentence when his patient appeared to look through him, "Is this too overwhelming to think about right now? I understand if you'd like to read a few books or get further information, but I really don't advise that you wait too long before starting on meds. The earlier in the bout, the better our chances for fighting it quickly."

Brenda's voice shook and her casual attitude left her, "I–I can't see a thing anymore, just flying colors. My eyes won't focus at all and I'm so dizzy and disoriented." Luke could see the fear that filled her and could hear that she struggled with the sudden blindness.

Brenda began to cry openly, not for her health, but for her seemingly ruined plans. "Doctor, I've known what I wanted since I was ten years old. I'm twenty-seven and I'm two years ahead of schedule; already a vice president. I never planned for any detours; illness isn't plausible." She paused for a moment and her tears stopped quickly. "I did allow for a sabbatical next year," she said eagerly. "Do you think this will last longer than two months?"

Luke tried to remain calm and kept his voice soothingly quiet, even as he reached for her elbow to guide her, ignoring her career-related questions. "It's all right, Brenda, it's probably just the stress of the diagnosis. It can leave as quickly as it comes. We're going to get you to the hospital right now. With your permission, I'm going to get you on intravenous steroids tonight."

"How long until I'm fat?" Brenda asked weakly.

Luke saw that Brenda Turner had it all in the world's eyes. Educated, successful, and beautiful. Of course, her appearance was important to her; it was probably a valuable asset to her success. He looked at the shapely woman with a man's eyes, her conditioned calf muscles were flexed sexily in her high heels and her tightly fitted cream skirt caressed her hourglass shape easily. "You shouldn't be on steroids long enough to gain weight." Catching himself he added, "Although, you can watch what you eat. And that does *not* mean diet. These medications will make you feel famished." He smiled at her and she returned a grateful grin.

"Thank you, Dr. Marcusson." Brenda's voice shook, her distinguishing confidence shattered.

"Do you have family or a friend who could bring your things to the hospital?" the doctor asked in his business tone, trying to sound unaffected by her answer.

"I'm not married and no one has a key to my home. How will I—" Brenda's anxious voice mounted with each statement. "Don't you understand? I don't have time for friends; I'm the vice president of marketing for Star Digital," she cried.

"So you've said." This woman baffled him with her devotion to a job; even for a nonbeliever. *If this woman would put her efforts toward God's work, who knows what she might accomplish?*

"Doctor, one day you will have video on demand. Any movie, anytime from the comfort of your own home. VCRs will be dinosaurs! My job is integral to making that dream a reality in America." Brenda's voice lifted with exuberance. Luke saw how her sales pitch had taken on a life of its own and her blindness seemed instantly forgotten.

"Since I don't own a television set, I'd say that dream is a little farther off for me than you might think. Now I want you in the hospital tonight. Will you agree to steroid treatment?"

"Seeing as how I can't see to drive, I'd say I have little choice. Would you mind calling me a cab?"

Luke knew by her request that her independence was past the point of healthy. He surprised himself by offering, "How about if I took you home? I know it's unorthodox, but I'd like you to start treatment as soon as possible." It wasn't one of his better ideas, but he wanted her to concentrate solely on getting better. He told himself to wrap himself in God's armor, for he was not blind to her appearance. He prayed silently for God's strength.

"Really? I just live here in Palo Alto, on Harding." Brenda placed her trust in Dr. Marcusson, allowing him to guide her toward his car.

æ

Brenda wasn't surprised by the doctor's offer. Men often went out of their way for her initially. Rarely, however, was she honored by a second invitation. Although her eyesight was now hopelessly blurred, she had a clear mental picture of the striking young doctor in his dark green golf shirt and his long legs in casual khakis. Dr. Marcusson guided her gently with large, refined hands. *Those of a surgeon,* she thought, marveling at his chivalry.

Once in the passenger seat, she fidgeted and felt her nylons catch on something. She moved and felt her stocking unravel down her calf. Seeing her confusion, the doctor apologized. "Oh, I'm sorry about that. I usually put a towel down when I'm expecting a passenger. The seat is ripped."

"What kind of car is this?" Brenda asked, her eyes unable to focus on the make.

"It's a '79 Pinto, complete with faux wood paneling exteriors, although they're pretty faded."

"You're kidding, right?" Brenda could not believe that someone with Luke Marcusson's credentials would drive a

Pinto by choice, and she laughed out loud at the notion.

"Just like television, cars aren't very important to me," he said seriously. With a certain horror, she realized he was telling the truth.

"I gather you're a single man, Dr. Marcusson," Brenda said, with mirth in her voice."

"As a matter of fact, I am. And the woman who takes me will have to love the Lord and my car," he stated playfully. "By the way, where on Harding?"

Brenda gave him directions and leaned back in her seat. She was intrigued. Surely, this man cared more for material items than he let on. *Doesn't everyone? Why would someone take the time to become a neurosurgeon when he apparently has no regard for possessions? On his salary, he could afford just about anything. Maybe he's some kind of monk. Why else would a man with a medical degree from Stanford believe in God? This guy does not compute.* Brenda found herself longing to know what made him tick.

"What do you do for excitement, Doctor? I take it you don't race this thing on weekends, and if you don't own a television, I guess you're not a couch potato." She knew by his sleek, athletic build that he wasn't one to sit around. Brenda felt light. While trying to decode her driver, she had completely forgotten that she was sightless. It almost made her game more fun. Blinded to his handsome profile, she wasn't intimidated by his clean, good looks, and it was easy to forget that he was a distinguished neurosurgeon.

"When I get a chance to get away, I generally work with my church's youth group. We take trips to the beach, mountain bike, and sometimes go camping. I haven't been as active lately though. I've had additional surgeries and a new research detail added to my schedule."

"No, I mean *fun*. What do you do for fun?" His angelic answers were beginning to annoy her and she felt trifled with by his eternal optimism.

"What do *you* do for fun, Miss Turner?" The question threw Brenda, who didn't have a valid answer herself.

"I don't really have much spare time, I'm vice. . ."

". . .president of marketing. Yes, I know." The doctor's voice was agitated and Brenda knew what she was up against now.

"I see. You're threatened by successful women. I don't see why you would be. You are a brain surgeon, I would think your ego could handle it." Brenda crossed her arms and rolled her blinded eyes.

Luke broke into uproarious laughter. "You pegged me."

His mocking laughter infuriated her and she persisted. "That's why you're religious, right? You're one of those radicals who use the Bible to keep a woman in her place. Home and pregnant! My parents were just like you, telling me all I needed was Jesus and a husband." Brenda could almost feel the steam coming from her ears. This man and his antiquated ideas caused her to fume; she thought they were extinct in Silicon Valley.

"Now, wait a minute," Luke stated calmly. "You can say a lot of things about me, but I would never use God's Word to do evil. Miss Turner, you may think God is a joke, but I assure you He is real. He loves you enough to have sent His only Son to die for you. Laugh at me all you want, but do yourself a favor: Read God's Word before you turn Him away."

Brenda shrank in her seat and felt her nylons rip up to her thigh. She told herself she shouldn't feel chastised by this zealot and yet his words cut her to the core. She stubbornly crossed her arms, knowing full well she had gone too far in her accusations. "I'm sorry, Dr. Marcusson. That was very rude," she said coldly. She wouldn't admit she was wrong, though; she still felt justified in her charges.

"You certainly seem to like a good fight, Miss Turner. Why don't you turn some of that energy toward your disease?"

Brenda was livid, but she knew he was right, which only made her angrier. He had pegged *her,* she did love a good fight. When she attended business meetings, she could debate anyone within shouting range, but she hadn't learned where to draw the line, the point where her words became weapons. Although men were quick to approach her, she rarely dated.

When she did, most were quickly put off by her opinionated manner. Brenda couldn't remember when there had been a second date. Fairly often, she was home by eight-thirty after the first one. She decided to try to put on her best behavior for the doctor. After all, Dr. Marcusson had graciously brought her home; she owed him her gratitude.

Luke pulled the car into the driveway and marveled aloud at her stylish Victorian home. "This is your house? It's pretty big for someone who lives alone. Well, I can't say environment has ever been too important to me. My nurse made me hire a designer for the office. She said she didn't want to spend all day in a place I designed. Imagine that," Luke joked, obviously trying to lighten the mood.

"I bought the place before the market took off. I've almost doubled my investment in five years. My mentor helped me get in, but I paid back every penny and my mortgage is quite reasonable, thanks to my bonuses. When Star goes public, I'll probably buy another house or duplex as an investment. I love real estate." Brenda couldn't imagine why she had allowed so much information to come tumbling out. Usually, she was quite particular about what she shared.

"That's wonderful. If I ever buy a place, I'll know who to. . ."

"You don't own a home?" Brenda was incredulous. "Dr. Marcusson, why don't you just hand the government your paycheck?" She stared in his direction, but between the looming darkness and her fuzzy eyesight, she couldn't even make out his imposing form. She imagined it, though.

"During my residency at Stanford, I moved into the campus housing and just never moved out. It's such a hassle to move. Besides, I spend so much time at the office and hospital, it's convenient living just across the street."

"Forget about convenience, we're going to find you a house. Even in this up market, I guarantee you'll be better off to purchase a home. I would imagine at your salary, you would need at least one tax shelter, probably more. When I have my eyesight back, we'll go house hunting." Brenda was shocked by her own forwardness and covered her mouth unconsciously, as though someone else had put the words there. Why had she so blatantly offered to spend time with him? No matter how attractive he was, his outdated morals made him clearly off-limits.

"Are you a real estate agent?" Luke asked innocently.

"Agent, in this area? Are you kidding? Everything's negotiable, Dr. Marcusson. Don't forget that. Do you know what six percent of a $600,000 house is? A ridiculous amount of money for filling out a few forms, that's what. This market is too expensive for a double realtor deal. Your closing costs would be outrageous."

Dr. Marcusson remained quiet and Brenda thought he didn't believe her. "I'm good at this, really, Doctor. I'll find you the best house in your price range, guaranteed. You're right that an agent is best if you're unsure of yourself, but when you've done it over and over again, they become obsolete. I can scan a contract faster than any agent I know. I guess it's kind of a hobby of mine; I just seem to have a sixth sense. I know what's out there and what's a good price." Brenda realized she must have sounded full of herself, but the fact was she did understand the real estate market and she loved house hunting. She had already helped several of her coworkers purchase homes.

"So that's what you do with your free time."

"I guess it is." Brenda delighted in the realization that she did have a hobby.

"If I decide to buy, you'll be the first to know. I'm trying to get a research fellowship at Baylor University in Texas right now. It's one of the best programs in the country and they may be close to the cure for multiple sclerosis."

Brenda had no idea why the thought of Luke Marcusson moving out of state bothered her, but it definitely did.

"Do you want help inside?" the doctor offered.

"No, I'll pack a few things and be out shortly." When Brenda fumbled with the car door, Luke reached across her and opened it. She felt his arm across her and her stomach fluttered at his touch. She wished he weren't so handsome, and found herself trying to concentrate on his chauvinistic attitudes. She stepped out onto her familiar driveway and the ground flew up to meet her with a hard bump.

≥∙

Luke watched her step from the car and disappear. He rushed out his door and ran to find her crumpled body on the driveway, her face looking shocked. "Are you okay?" he asked.

"I'll take that hand after all, Dr. Marcusson." As Luke lifted her from the concrete her warm scent filled his senses. He closed his eyes and allowed the moment to overwhelm him before he remembered that she was his patient. He had no business being at her home, but how could he have allowed her to go alone in a cab? He might have called his cousin Katie, her secretary, but that would have broken patient confidentiality.

Clearly, God had led him there and now he would have to be worthy of the call. He straightened and took a step back while still holding firmly onto her arms to help her balance. Walking backward, he led her up the steps to her wide front porch. Proverbs 31, where God describes a godly wife, suddenly popped into his mind, along with a new insight. A desirable woman that needed him was certainly more temptation than he was capable of handling alone. He remembered the verse about beauty being fleeting and now fully understood its meaning. This woman was truly captivating.

Luke had always imagined his future wife would be the sweet, gentle soul that relished being a wife and mother. Surely, Brenda Turner held no stock in such values and he found himself annoyed that he didn't know better than to be attracted to her.

Brenda reached into her soft leather briefcase and came up with a set of keys. Luke took them from her and unlocked the door, "Where's the light?"

"To your right, there's a switch on the wall." He reached in and soon the front porch and living room were awash with light. Brenda stumbled in before him, a pleasant smile crossing her face. "Home at last."

Luke breathed deeply to take in the scent of vanilla. He was surprised at the warmth of Brenda's home. Luke had expected her home to be filled with cold, modern furnishings. He was fascinated to find her entire home Victorian in theme. A traditional, white crown molding lined the walls at both the ceiling and the floor. The room was painted a deep, muted lavender and the sofas were white tapestry with dark, Queen Anne legs that matched the hardwood floors throughout the home. "I feel like I've stepped back in time. Lavender . . .hmm. It's really very nice."

"Ralph Lauren," she said, while placing her keys back in her satchel.

"Lauren Bacall."

"What?" Brenda missed his joke.

"Aren't we naming famous people?"

"No. I was telling you the designer of the paint color."

"Ah. . .so it would have been more appropriate for me to say Sherwin-Williams?"

"You have a strange sense of humor, Doctor. Make yourself at home, I'm going to crash into the bedroom and get my things. Open the armoire there and you'll find a big, black box. It's called a television. On the coffee table, there's a little box called a remote. There are sixty different channels waiting to entertain you."

"Channels? I thought the future of television was that I get to choose anything."

"Only if you make me well, so I can implement it. In case no one informed you, I'm vice president of marketing." She winked at him and felt her way into the bedroom.

Luke looked around the room with interest. The focal point of the room was a large marble fireplace, surrounded by a white mantel on three sides. The marble continued onto the floor in a splash of gray. On the mantel were two antique, silver frames and Luke walked toward them to study the contents. He noticed immediately to his satisfaction that there were no men in the pictures.

"Who's this little girl?" Luke called toward the bedroom. He kept his voice low, because everything echoed over the hardwood floors.

"On the mantel? That's my niece, Kaitlyn. I've never seen her in person, she lives back east with my brother and his wife."

"That's too bad. You certainly put some thought into decorating. Are these all antiques?"

"Not all of them, but I take my vacations down south to purchase antiques and furniture. For some reason, it's just easier for me to take a vacation if I have a goal in mind." Brenda emerged from the hallway with a small overnight bag that matched her briefcase.

She was charmingly adorned in a fitted pair of jeans and a white tee shirt. Luke could not remember when he'd seen such justice done to a pair of Levi's. His doctor's eyes failed him once again and he knew that having Brenda Turner as a patient was playing with fire.

"Dr. Marcusson? Are you there?" She asked anxiously, a worried frown crossing her beautiful, full lips.

"Over here, Miss Turner." Luke walked toward her as he spoke, giving her a general idea of his location. "You certainly look more relaxed. How on earth did you get ready so fast?"

"I'm not very patient, so I know how to do things quickly. I keep an overnight bag packed at all times. I never know when I'll get called away on business. I have a suit and a pair of casual clothes packed. I just took the suit out."

"Very organized, I'm impressed."

"Doctor Marcusson, what if these steroids don't work? I've got to work to support myself. It's not only my life, it's my livelihood we're talking about."

"We'll deal with each problem as it comes, okay? In the meantime, I think we're going to have excellent luck with the corticosteroid therapy, and there are many new therapies becoming available that help to prevent new exacerbations, and the cure gets closer every day. Let me take your bag and you hang on to my arm. Is there anyone you need to call before we go?"

"Just my secretary, Katie. She'll need to know I won't be in tomorrow. This is such bad timing, I've got a deadline. I have all the necessary files with me, the office will be at a standstill." Brenda shook her head, clearly disturbed.

Luke quickly changed the subject, "I think it's only fair to tell you that Katie goes to my church. She's also my cousin." Luke spoke in a quiet whisper now that Brenda was on his arm.

She looked at the floor and shook her head. "When you started talking religion, I had an inkling you two knew each other."

Luke ignored her comment and continued, "I'll call her after you're checked into the hospital and let her know you will be out for a while with doctor's orders."

"But I don't want her. . ."

"I wouldn't tell her of your condition without your approval."

≈

Dr. Marcusson checked Brenda into her room and a nurse started an IV immediately. "Miss Turner, this may give you trouble sleeping and I noticed you brought your briefcase with you, but I want to make it clear: No reading. Do you understand?" Brenda just nodded in reluctant agreement. "I'm not telling you this to punish you. . ."

"You have no idea what you're asking me to do. My eyes are my life. I am successful because of them. I. . ."

He cut her off quickly, "Hopefully, that won't change after therapy, but you must allow yourself to get better or you may not fully recover. Okay?" Luke felt like he was talking to a child, but he also knew this was one obstinate woman. The way she looked at him so expectantly with her tropical blue eyes sent his emotions soaring. He shook the thought. As much as he found himself attracted to her, he found himself equally exasperated by her intense preoccupation with her job.

"Yes, Doctor," Brenda sang in a sarcastic tone.

"I'll have the nurse get some books on tape from the hospital library. What do you like to read?"

"The classics."

"You're determined to make my day tough, aren't you?"

"Don't you mean night?" Brenda asked. "It must be well past nine by now."

"You're right, I need to get something to eat and turn in for the night. I'll see you in the morning during my rounds. If you need anything, your call button is right here." Luke took her hand and placed it on the button. Her warm touch electrified him. He held her hand a moment longer than necessary and pried himself away from her bedside. "Good night, Brenda," he whispered.

"Good night Luke," she answered quietly after he'd left.

three

Brenda awoke the next morning after a few hours of restless slumber. The medicine had made falling asleep nearly impossible, but the drastic fatigue of MS finally prevailed. When she opened her eyes, a whirlwind of colors whizzed by and she instantly dissolved to tears. Her eyesight had not returned, and for the first time, Brenda realized she might not recover. Her first thought was of her beloved Victorian home. *I must get better,* she vowed. With renewed determination she thought about the campaign she had to complete. She rang for a nurse to dial her direct line at Star Digital.

"Katie, this is Brenda." She struggled with her emotions. Dr. Marcusson had said the drugs would cause her to be overly sensitive. Inwardly, she hoped this was the only reason she seemed unable to maintain a steady voice.

"Brenda, I'm so happy to hear your voice. Are you all right? Luke. . .I mean, Dr. Marcusson called me last night to let me know you weren't feeling well. Is there anything I can do?"

"Katie, I'm fine. I'm just having a little trouble with my eyesight. Dr. Marcusson is wonderful. Thank you for recommending him."

"He's not too bad on the eyes either, huh?" Katie joked and Brenda felt her stomach turn.

"They've got different patches and things on my eyes all the time, so I'm afraid his looks are lost on me." Brenda lied without the slightest hint of guilt. She had managed to keep her blindness under wraps, as well as her attraction to the handsome doctor.

"Can I bring you anything? A mocha and a Balance bar perhaps?" Katie asked and Brenda laughed at the reference to her normal morning snack.

"The breakfast of champions? No, thanks. They're treating me fine here."

"Now I know you're ill. When *you* consider hospital food fine treatment, something's not right."

Brenda ignored the comment. "Katie, I need you to do something for me. I need you to take the campaign on my desk to Mike Wilcox." Brenda cringed with the words. Mike had been her fierce competitor since she started in Star's marketing department three years ago. She had won the coveted vice president's position, but Mike was always lurking, waiting for her to fail. She knew this was his opportunity, yet there was nothing she could do about it. She was of no use without her eyesight, but she couldn't allow Star Digital to fail at such a crucial time. She took solace in having the most pertinent files in her briefcase stashed safely under the bed.

"Mike Wilcox? But, Brenda he'll take credit for everything you've done."

"I know, Katie, but he's also the only one who can meet my deadline." Brenda began crying suddenly. Relinquishing her responsibilities made the loss of her eyesight a stinging reality. A flood of tears followed and she sniffled loudly into the phone, unable to maintain decorum. "Oh, Katie, I have to go now. They want to do more tests." Brenda hung up the phone before Katie could respond and covered her face while she sobbed.

"Miss Turner?" Dr. Marcusson's familiar voice was soft and low and soon Brenda felt his consoling hand on her shoulder. Unconsciously placing her hand on top of his, she sniffled, hiccuped, and continued crying.

"I can't see!" she wailed.

"I know—I know, but that's why you're here." He slipped his hand from beneath hers and she knew he must be looking at her. She must have appeared a sight. She squeezed her eyes shut, as though that would make her invisible.

"I love to read. I read *everything*. How will I live without it? Or drive? Or work. . .what if I can't go back to work? I could lose everything. My entire life feels over."

Dr. Marcusson didn't respond at first and Brenda reached with her hand to make sure he was still there. "Miss Turner, the chances of you losing your eyesight permanently are very remote. We're doing everything we can and once you can see again we'll talk about options for reducing future episodes. Open your eyes and look toward me."

Brenda pulled back to look up at the doctor, but grasped firmly onto his hands to secure his presence. She saw a flurry of color pass by and the mere act of opening her eyes made her stomach nauseous again. "You're wearing white and you're on the ceiling and floor." She laughed through her tears and she felt him squeeze her hands gently.

"You're right, I am wearing white, it's a lab coat. Since you can't read right now I'm going to tell you some of the basics of MS. Bouts typically last eight weeks at this stage. Let's just look at that as our deadline for now, okay?"

"Eight weeks, right," Brenda said aloud, mentally counting the days.

"Miss Turner, I can't promise you what course your disease will take, but I've talked to a friend. She's agreed to dictate a book on the subject onto a cassette tape. I'm picking her up at the airport tonight and she promised to have it done by the end of the weekend."

Brenda missed the message regarding the book. All she heard was that Luke was picking up a woman at the airport. Jealousy shot through her like a bolt of lightning and instinctively she asked to know more.

"A friend?" she asked slyly.

"Actually, it's my ex-fiancée. We're still good friends. She's just getting back from the mission field in Africa." Dr. Marcusson's tone told her he admired his ex-fiancée's work and Brenda felt overwhelmingly empty. If Dr. Marcusson liked women who did charity work, Brenda had nothing to offer. Everything she did in life was based on a return for her investment, both for her time and money.

"Why didn't you get married?" Brenda tried to sound casual,

but feared her interest was altogether transparent.

"We just felt God was leading us in different directions."

"You think God talks to you?" she asked honestly.

"I know He does. That doesn't mean He calls my name out loud or that I hear voices. It means He speaks to me through prayer, the church, my close friends, and in circumstances. Understand?"

"No." Brenda shook her head. She wanted to say she did. She was sure his ex-fiancée heard God too, and her competitive nature wanted to lie to him, but somehow she couldn't.

"Dr. Marcusson?" A nurse appeared in the doorway. Brenda sensed a white outline in the lighted hallway and it angered her. She knew Luke would be called away.

"Yes," he answered.

"Wyatt Ross is on the line for you. She says her plane will be in early. This afternoon at two. If you can make it, great. Otherwise, she says she'll grab a taxi."

"Thank you, nurse. I'll be there. Would you mind giving her the message?"

"Certainly, Doctor." Brenda saw the doorway darken and she relished once again being alone with Dr. Marcusson. She wondered why he could leave in the middle of the day to pick up an old girlfriend at the airport, but couldn't see new patients for over a month. She glared at him warily, envying the woman that wielded such power over him.

"Is my car safe at your office?" Brenda wanted to kick herself. His selfless ex-fiancée was returning from the deserts of Africa, and here *she* was asking about her BMW.

"Of course it's safe, but I can store it at my place if it makes you feel better."

"Would you mind?" Brenda liked the idea of her car being at the doctor's house. It made her feel she was more than just his patient.

"I want you to forget about things like your car. They're unimportant. Your assignment today is to listen to a soap opera, Oprah, or something equally brain-draining and tell me what happened, okay? They'll be starting your IV earlier today, so I hope it won't affect your sleep as much. I've pre-scribed a sedative if you need it. 'Til tomorrow. . ."

"You're not coming back today?" Fear filled her voice.

"I have a full set of rounds to make and other patients to see. Let me know what Oprah has to say." He patted her shoulder and walked from the room, leaving Brenda feeling utterly abandoned.

◆

Luke had crammed all of his appointments into the morning to accommodate Wyatt's arrival at the airport. His present surgery and patient schedule felt like his residency and it was begin-ning to take its toll. He had already spent far too much time with Brenda Turner, but he couldn't help himself. He wanted her to know that no matter how bad things got, God would be there for her and so would he. However, he knew his own emotions were becoming entangled and he longed to discuss them openly with Wyatt, his confidante.

He arrived at the airport and parked close to the terminal. He was glad she had chosen to fly into the San Jose airport, which was far more accessible than San Francisco International. He found Wyatt's flight number on a screen and rushed to meet the on-time flight. When he approached the gate, Wyatt's tanned face, under an untamed mane of light brown hair, beamed with a welcoming smile.

"Luke, I'm so glad you could come. I can't wait to tell you about my trip. We treated and healed hundreds with the medi-cine that was provided. What a blessing." Wyatt's enthusiasm was obvious and Luke felt a tinge of envy. "Luke? What's the matter with you?"

Luke laughed. Wyatt was always so perceptive and at times it unnerved him. "The patient I told you about on the phone last night."

"Brenda? I've been praying for her."

"There's something more. I'm drawn to her like a magnet, even though she's not a Christian," he confessed. "As a matter of fact, her only religion seems to be financial success."

"Do you think treating her is too much of a temptation?"

Wyatt put a concerned arm around him.

"She's gorgeous, Wyatt, but her heart is so hardened. I wish I could help her myself. I see this scared little girl that I just want to rescue and care for. She doesn't seem to have any friends and her only concern seems to be for her work and possessions. I'm embarrassed to admit how attracted I am to her. How much I want to be there for her. We're nothing alike, she loves the things of this world, while I love the people in it. Still. . .there's something in her eyes that speaks to me."

"Don't be too hard on yourself, Luke. Maybe you see something deeper. If it were just her looks, I don't think you'd spend so much time thinking about her welfare. After all, a pretty, blind woman in love with *things* doesn't sound all that attractive. Perhaps God has given you a special calling regarding her. Some of the hardest hearts are the easiest to crack open with His unconditional love. Have you prayed about your feelings?"

"Constantly, but so far, God is quiet. Pretty comical considering I just told her today how God speaks to me. I've only known her two days, but her case just consumes me."

"Maybe if you allow others to take on some of the burden, you'll feel less passionate about the case. I finished the translating the book for her on the plane." Wyatt held up a cassette tape.

"How could you possibly. . ."

"Your voice sounded pretty urgent last night so I borrowed a book from the medical library in Kigali. I can't sleep on planes anyway. My neighbors didn't exactly appreciate my constant talking into the tape recorder, but if anyone they know gets MS, they'll be prepared."

"You must be exhausted. Let's get you home. Besides, Brenda probably will take to the steroids and be out of my life for good within a week. When's Barry arriving?"

"He's coming Saturday. He managed to rummage some additional meds in town and stayed to administer them. He's speaking at our church on Sunday, trying to drum up some more support so we can go back soon. We want to try to stay for good this time, so funding will be more difficult."

"I've got to hand it to you, Wyatt. You and that husband of yours sure have hearts for the sick and needy."

"So do you, Doctor. Your calling just pays better." She laughed an infectious giggle. "Luke, God has you here for a reason." She paused for a moment and looked into his troubled eyes, "Perhaps Miss Brenda Turner is that reason."

Luke smiled at the mention of the name and lifted the string-wrapped boxes that served as Wyatt's makeshift luggage. He had driven Brenda's car to pick up Wyatt and now was embarrassed at the showiness of the vehicle. Wyatt was awestruck. "You got rid of the Pinto?"

"I'll get rid of the Pinto when one too many parts has to be scraped off the pavement. This is Brenda's. She was worried about leaving it in the parking lot and I told her I would park it at my campus apartment. I figured my car would be safe in the parking lot."

"Unless they tow it as an abandoned vehicle." They laughed together and Luke's heart lifted. He was truly glad he had remained friends with Wyatt Ross. They had been school-mates since childhood in Christian school. They had always talked of marriage, but when it came down to actually going through with it, they realized the love they shared was not for marriage. It was always more of a mutual admiration.

He had been thrilled when she married his fellow neurologist Barry Ross. Now the couple came home twice a year for fund-raising and then went off to Africa to treat the ill, both with prayer and medication.

"Listen, smart alec. That vehicle has picked you up many a time. You and Barry should be grateful for my faithful chariot," Luke chastised.

"Yeah, well that 'chariot' has also left us stranded on many a street, or have you conveniently forgotten?"

"Always looking at the negative." Luke clicked his tongue.

Wyatt's tone turned serious. "Luke, I'm going to drop by and meet Brenda tomorrow. It sounds like she needs a friend. I'll let her know I'm a nurse, would that be okay?"

"That'd be great. I'm anxious to hear your opinion. Perhaps, you'll see that same special spark that I see."

The two sped off in the BMW while Wyatt filled Luke in on her latest mission trip.

four

Brenda awoke early to the sound of her roommate's blaring television set. *Is this woman deaf?* She roughly pulled the sheet over her head and turned over, but it was no use. A news anchor's peppy voice boomed with authority through the thin curtain separating the two beds.

"Brenda? Are you in here?"

"Katie?" Brenda recognized her secretary's voice and its familiarity made her want to cry with joy. She had been in the hospital for three days now and she was lonely. No one had come to visit, which was no surprise; but in her shattered state, it cut deeply. Brenda's only living relatives were her brother and grandparents in Connecticut and they wouldn't care. "What time is it?" she asked groggily as she sat up in bed.

"It's 7:30 on Saturday morning. I brought you a mocha and a Balance bar." Katie's thoughtfulness proved too much and Brenda's eyes began watering. She felt Katie's arms around her and she cried softly into her shoulder.

When she finally was able to speak, she began slowly, "I can't see anything but flying colors. Dr. Marcusson says I have multiple sclerosis." It was the first time she'd said it, and the admission made it a stark reality.

"It's okay, Brenda. I'm here and God is here." Katie placed her hands on Brenda's slender, elegantly manicured hands while she talked. "Jesus healed a blind man in the New Testament; I brought my Bible if you'd like to hear about it," Katie said brightly.

"I don't think so, Katie. Thanks." Brenda nodded her head negatively, but Katie seemed undeterred.

"He has the power to heal you, Brenda, but even if He doesn't, He will give you the strength to go through it. Lean on Him. You won't be alone; I'm here, and you've got the best doctor in Silicon Valley, I made sure of that." Katie's easy reference to God was unusually comforting to Brenda. Usually, the young executive balked at Katie's insipid prayer talk, but today it was soothing and even seemed to make sense. Still, it left her with more questions than answers.

"I bet Mike Wilcox was drooling over being handed the campaign. I've worked so hard on this stupid project; I just want to hurt something." Brenda hit the bed dramatically, startling the woman in the next bed.

"Brenda, let it go. Concentrate on getting better. Mike Wilcox sees the void he's been waiting for. No offense, but you would do the same thing."

"Ouch," Brenda said, chastened by her assistant's candor.

"Well?" Katie said, her arms crossed, anticipating the answer.

"Okay, you're right, I would." Brenda quickly added, "But that doesn't make it right."

"No it doesn't, but you've played this game long enough to know business sometimes has nothing to do with what's right. I want you to stop worrying about work. It's only a job, and you'll be back before you know it."

"When Star Digital has its initial public stock offering, I'll be rich!" Enthusiasm rippled through Brenda's voice. "That opportunity doesn't present itself at every company, you know. I started on the ground floor of this company, I deserve that money."

"You own a half-million dollar house in Palo Alto, it's full of antiques, and you have a BMW convertible. What more do you need?"

The question threw her for a moment. "Katie, the house is worth $600,000, and I *could* own two, or maybe three, as investments." Brenda was boggled by Katie's lack of understanding. Surely, everyone wanted more, that was the American way.

"Brenda, just for your benefit, I'm nodding my head and crossing my arms in disgust. Since you can't see me, I want you to know how sick you sound and it has *nothing* to do with being in this hospital. God has already given you so much. . ."

"God gave me this stupid disease and now all the money I earned is just slipping through my fingers." Brenda's voice dripped with self-pity.

"Disease?" Katie said sharply. "Brenda, how dare you blame God for this disease and not thank Him for everything else. Life is not always perfect, you know. If you're going to acknowledge God, you need to remember His goodness first. You've never thanked Him for all His provisions, but once a tiny spoke gets thrown in your wheel, it's all God's fault."

"Tiny spoke?" Brenda snorted. "I have *multiple sclerosis,* a chronic illness that is *attacking* my body. I may be like this forever. I have no husband to support me, no one to pay my mortgage. I'm all I have, I make it happen."

"Brenda, I know you don't feel well. And I know it's scary that your eyes aren't functioning, but your real sickness is inside. God has provided for you all along. Even now, He's given you a survivor personality, a hospital and doctor providing the best of care, and people who *want* to help. So stop concentrating on what you don't have and start concentrating on what you do."

Katie had always been blunt with Brenda, but never this candid. The executive flinched as though the words were daggers. All Brenda wanted was a little compassion, but her assistant seemed oblivious. Just like her mother always had. *Religious people just don't get it.*

"Katie, you don't understand. You're one of those people that life comes easy for. You see the best in all situations, no matter what. I'm not built to be content. That's why I'm so good at what I do." *You probably don't even care about a nice house,* she thought. *You can't understand because material possessions aren't important to you. If they were, you would have gotten a better education, and you'd be more than just a stupid marketing assistant.* Brenda crossed her arms and leaned back on her pillow like an angry, spoiled child.

"How's my favorite patient?" Luke Marcusson's lighthearted voice broke the tension in the room and Brenda grinned widely at his presence, instantly forgetting the confrontation.

"Tired and grumpy," Katie replied.

"Steroids can certainly bring out the best in a person." Luke laughed at the remark, but inwardly Brenda was grateful for the diversion.

"Thanks for the excuse, Dr. Marcusson, but I'm afraid Katie knew me before the steroids," Brenda reluctantly admitted.

They all shared in the joke before the doctor began asking about Brenda's vision. "Brenda, can you look in my direction?" Brenda looked toward the deep voice and for a fleeting moment saw the gorgeous man she remembered. His tall stature and rugged jawline immediately had her full attention.

She watched him move his clean, flawless hands to rub his face and immediately began to dream of them. She always noticed a man's hands and Luke's were seemingly perfect, large and masculine, yet sleek and graceful enough to perform surgery. Brenda found herself swept away in her thoughts before she realized she was actually *seeing* the dream before her.

"I see you!" she said excitedly. "You're still jumping toward the ceiling, but I can see your features—and your hands," she added shyly, as though he might read her thoughts. Dr. Marcusson held his finger above her head and asked her to track it. She tried, but it made her eyes hurt with the strain and she closed them tightly.

"Brenda, the steroids seem to be working. Tomorrow, I'm going to switch you to oral steroids and send you home. I'd rather you not be alone, at least for a few days. Do you have someone who can stay with you?" Again, Brenda cringed at the thought that she had no friends. She certainly didn't want to admit such a thing twice to Luke Marcusson, and her mind reeled for an alternative.

"I can hire a nurse. I wouldn't want to put anyone out."

"Nonsense, Brenda. You'll stay with Jacob and me," Katie offered in her perky voice.

Brenda felt trapped. If she said yes, Dr. Marcusson would know she was fresh out of friends. What would he think of her? If she said no, she had the added stress of finding a nurse quickly. "No, Katie, I couldn't. I wouldn't want to impose." Brenda longed to go home alone, but she knew without her complete eyesight and faculties, she needed help. Brenda's lack of friends left few alternatives. She felt the doctor looking at her, probably wondering what kind of woman would be so pathetically alone in the overpopulated Silicon Valley.

"Impose? In our house? There is no such word. I'll pick you up and we'll go by your house first and get your things. When can she go, Dr. Luke?"

"This afternoon, right after her IV treatment. I'll release her about 1:30," Luke said decisively. Brenda couldn't help but wonder whether this had been planned, but knowing Katie's inability to lie, she doubted they could have pulled off such an elaborate ruse.

"Great, we'll get home in time for Oprah," Katie joked. Luke and Katie planned the next few days, while Brenda sat idly by, relinquishing control of her life.

five

Brenda kept her eyes closed on the ride home, which saved her from the constant blur of the passing sights. She relished the warm sunlight and smiled at the thought of home. When she arrived at the stately Victorian, the wild jumping in her vision was beginning to settle down; she was definitely getting better.

Once inside, her beloved dining room set from South Carolina came into view. She walked toward it and gently touched her precious English china displayed on the elaborate mahogany sideboard. Seeing her treasures made her eyes water. *These are my friends*—the perfected surroundings she had worked so long and diligently to create. She ran her fingers along the table, grateful to be home.

As she stood in the entryway between the dining room and the living room, she heard Katie come up behind her. "Brenda, do you need help?"

"No, no. Just thinking about a few friends." Brenda knew she related better to objects than to people, but her elegant furniture was of little use to her now. *Katie is the only one here for me and maybe that's because she fears for her job.* Brenda's eyes welled up. "These medications have me on a roller coaster," she said, by way of an excuse.

"You'll be home to stay in just a few days. I know our home isn't yours, but we'll love having you." The petite brunette craned her neck to look into her boss's eyes.

Brenda nodded and took new courage as she walked further into the house to gather her things. The message light blinked on the answering machine and she tentatively pushed the button. "Yeah, Brenda. Mike Wilcox here. Looking for the prep sheets on the campaign for the set-top boxes. Call me." Beep.

"Miss Turner. This is Wells Fargo Bank calling to inform

you that you are qualified for our new platinum Visa card. We'll call later." Beep.

"Hi, Brenda, it's Chris at Slatterly Antiques. Just found a beauty of a Queen Anne buffet. Looks just like you and I won't put it on the floor until Monday. Call me if you're interested." Beep.

Painfully, it was true. No one cared that her eyesight was precarious. She slowly packed her things and walked gloomily out to Katie's car.

"Is everything okay, Brenda?"

"This disease has opened my eyes about a few things," Brenda said cryptically.

"Nothing like slowing down to discover our true selves," Katie offered discerningly.

The ride to Katie's house was mostly silent, each woman lost in her own thoughts. When Brenda realized where they were headed she spoke up loudly. "Where do you live?" she asked nervously.

"EPA."

"East Palo Alto? *Murder capital of the United States, East Palo Alto!*"

"That was a long time ago. Not since 1992, in fact. Things have calmed down a lot since then. There was heavy gang activity that year; a lot of retaliation gunfire."

"Uh, Katie. We're talking death here. Surely, you make enough to live in a decent part of town."

"My husband and I have a ministry here. Jacob's a lay pastor, been working with some of these kids for nearly ten years. Long before we were married. Now some of them are grown and married themselves."

Katie's romantic reminiscence was lost on Brenda. "Don't you know what people think about this city? How can you possibly live here?" Brenda was truly frightened to be heading into such a notorious place. She had lived in the Bay Area for a decade and never once driven through the dangerous neighborhood.

"That's perception, not reality. This is a very tight-knit

community and people really care about each other. I have no fear for my safety here; neighbors look out for one another. Of course, there are certain areas I don't wander into that are known gang turf, but our neighborhood is perfectly safe. Besides, my fate is secure in Christ."

Brenda remained unfazed by the romanticized description. After all, she read the newspaper and she knew what went on in East Palo Alto: drug deals and murders. Katie drove deeper into the shabby neighborhood. Brenda strained to see the worn-out houses with their unkempt yards and discarded cars where there should have been lawn. Her fearful eyes were drawn to the black iron bars guarding each window and doorway. People of all descriptions stood on the street corners and in the front yards; their sheer number was enough to intimidate a passerby.

"See what I mean, Brenda? It's Saturday and everyone is out socializing. Up here on your right, this local church has a barbecue every weekend to raise money. Can you smell it?" Katie was her usual upbeat self and Brenda stared at her as though she were crazy.

"Katie, I don't think these guys are socializing. They're probably organizing a drive-by shooting or something."

"Brenda Turner, you watch too many movies. Just because people are poor does *not* mean they're criminals. I know for a fact they are socializing. Usually on Saturday, I'm out here with them. Stay with us a few days and you'll learn to look beyond someone's outward appearance or the car they drive."

Brenda rolled her eyes at Katie's naiveté; her religious lifestyle surely clouded her judgment. The car pulled into a driveway and Brenda was shocked at the darling house that fluttered slowly in her gradually returning vision. It was blue and white with a picket fence in front and flower boxes hanging from each window. The porch had a white wooden swing dangling contentedly from its roof and a tiny, child-size rocking chair beside it.

"Stay in the car, I'll come around and get you," Katie demanded. Brenda wanted to say there was no way she'd leave the car without a bulletproof vest, but decided it was better not to offend her hostess any further.

The car door opened and a tall, mustached man with light, wavy hair stood above her with his hand extended. He had a certain sweetness in his face and his smile was warm and genuine. "I'm Jacob Cummings. It's such a pleasure to finally meet you. Katie just goes on and on about you; I feel like I know you already."

Brenda took the extended hand and unfolded herself out of the vehicle. Katie came and stood next to her husband and peered up at him with admiring eyes. Brenda envied the love Katie so obviously felt for Jacob. *Will I ever find a love like that, where I can look at a man with such awe and respect?* She snapped back to reality; certainly she wasn't the type for dreamy-eyed looks and romantic fantasies. "Jacob, I can't thank you enough. I'm sure Katie's told you that I can be difficult. I appreciate your taking me in, anyway."

"On the contrary, Brenda. Katie has nothing but praise for you. You're always welcome in our home." An African-American boy with big, full cheeks peered between Jacob's tall legs and looked up at Brenda. "This is Daydan, he's three and he lives here with us." The boy smiled a wily grin and held up three small fingers.

"I didn't know," Brenda said absently.

"You never asked, I guess." Katie hadn't meant the words as a reprimand, but Brenda rarely took an interest in others. She was simply too busy at work for idle chitchat.

"Let's get you settled so you can rest. I understand you have orders to watch Oprah." Brenda laughed and allowed her things to be taken to a bedroom in the rear of the house. Daydan followed behind Katie and Jacob, leaving Brenda alone in the living room.

The interior of the house was quaint and warm. French blue carpet provided a country feel and Katie's many crafts filled the walls: homemade dolls, patchwork quilts, and several tole paintings which left little room for future projects.

Brenda smiled to herself, because her eyes were slowly

returning to normal and she could see the simple decorations. Their presence took on added meaning as she saw things she would normally have ignored for their lack of elegance. The furniture was simple and functional with heavy oak pieces taking up the bulk of the room. A boxy, dark oak armoire stood in the corner with a television. The sofas were a dark blue check and a country red rocking chair completed the grouping.

Brenda stretched her worn frame. Her body ached from fatigue and her eyes stung from wearied dryness. The medication made it impossible to relax, although she shuddered with exhaustion. Even though she was slowly regaining her eyesight, she was beginning to wonder at what price.

Katie returned to the living room with Daydan in tow and sat on the couch. "Can I get you anything to drink or eat? I stocked up on Balance bars and diet Pepsi, but I'm assuming you eat real food too."

"Momma Katie, I hungry," Daydan replied.

"He talks?" Brenda asked.

"Of course he talks, he's three years old," Katie answered incredulously.

"I've never really spent much time around children," Brenda shrugged.

"I'm sorry, Brenda. That was rude. I just spend so much time around them that I forget it isn't obvious to everyone. Daydan, Daddy went out back. Why don't you go see if you can help him in the yard? Then I'll have a snack for you when you come back."

"Okay, bye-bye." The boy waved at Brenda and she returned the gesture with a smile.

"Brenda, about Daydan; he is our son. His mother was a teenager in our weekly Bible study about four years ago; Tasha was her name. She dropped out of the class, but returned after Daydan was born. She was obviously on drugs, but asked if she could leave Daydan for an afternoon while she went to see about a job." Katie's eyes began welling up with tears and Brenda felt helpless at the sight, wondering if she should do something for her friend, but she remained in her seat like a wooden doll. "Anyway," Katie continued through her tears, "that was two and a half years ago. We've raised Daydan as our own since he was six months old. His grandmother, Ruth, helped us get temporary custody because she was too old to watch him all the time. While we work, Ruth takes him during the day. We've just been notified that Tasha has completed a drug treatment program and may be allowed to regain custody within the next few months." Katie was choking over her sobs now. "I know you have enough to think about, Brenda, and I don't mean to bring you lower, but I love that boy as if he were my own flesh, and I am going to fight for him with everything I have. I'm telling you this so that you know that Daydan doesn't leave with anyone. Okay?"

"Of course, Katie. Absolutely." Brenda's heart ached at the story of her assistant's plight. Katie had never brought it up or had an outburst at work. Brenda hadn't even known the child was Katie's, although the dozens of pictures on the secretary's desk would have made it clear to anyone who had bothered to inquire.

The fact that Katie would take Brenda in at such a difficult time seemed unreal. *Why would anyone take energy reserved for a custody battle and throw it away on me? She seems to have complete self-control. I wish I could approach work in such a quiet manner; that kind of poker face is worth millions.* Brenda longed to know Katie's secret, but knew it wasn't the time to ask. She placed her hand awkwardly on Katie's back and began to pat it softly.

☙

Luke rubbed his tired eyes with the palms of his cramped, postsurgery hands. He cradled his head while he bent over a plate of dried meatloaf and instant mashed potatoes in the hospital cafeteria.

"Luke?"

The young doctor looked up to see Wyatt Ross standing over him with a small, clear plastic bag filled with tapes. "I came for Brenda, but it seems she's checked out. I have all this MS information for her."

"Of course, Wyatt. Sit down. I released her today after treatment." Luke motioned with his hand for Wyatt to sit as he stood up. "Do you want a cup of coffee?"

"I don't need a thing, Luke. Please sit down, you look half-dead."

"I feel half-dead. I've had so many surgeries scheduled this past week and dozens of research patients to see before tomorrow. I ought to have that fellowship at Baylor within three months."

"How is Brenda?" Wyatt asked.

Luke's heart jumped at the mention of her name, but he maintained his even physician's voice. The image of Brenda's beautiful, deep-blue eyes and tangled blond hair danced in his mind's eye. "She's slowly regaining her eyesight. I think within a few weeks, she'll be back to normal."

Wyatt wasn't fooled by his casual answer, "I guess what I meant was how are *you* and Brenda doing? Have you had a chance to reconcile your feelings?"

"I've had a few days to pray over the matter and I've decided to transfer her case to another neurologist." Luke looked away.

"I think that's the right thing to do, Luke," she said placidly.

"I'm handing her case over because I can't see her with physician's eyes. The sooner she's on her way, the better," he lied. "She may help me with finding a house," he added quietly.

"I thought your future was in Texas at Baylor. Sounds like your grasping at straws, Luke," Wyatt said honestly.

"Bay Area real estate is a good investment, regardless. I could always rent it out," Luke offered weakly. Deep in his heart, he knew it wasn't a good idea to spend time with Brenda. It would only allow his feelings for her to deepen, but he also didn't want to think about never seeing her again. There was just something about her, something about *them*. "Besides, I didn't ask if it was a good idea. I need a tax write-off and she's going to help," Luke snapped, cutting off further discussion.

"Okay, fine." Wyatt raised her palms in surrender. "Let's

change the subject, shall we? This one is becoming a little volatile for my taste. Where is Brenda? I'd like to get her these tapes."

"She's at Katie's," Luke grumbled.

"In East Palo Alto?" Wyatt asked in disbelief.

"Yes." Luke knew he was being cold with Wyatt, but he also knew their friendship could withstand the temporary freeze. He wasn't in the mood for explaining himself. All he wanted to do was find a doctor's cot and lie down.

"See you at church tomorrow," Wyatt said kindly.

Luke realized Wyatt's feelings were hurt. As she walked away he added, "Thanks, Wyatt. I'm sorry I snapped at you."

"Barry and I only want what's best for you, Luke. You know that."

Luke just nodded.

&

"Will you read me a story?" Daydan asked, his huge brown eyes open wide in anticipation.

Brenda looked down at the tiny boy that appeared by her side on the sofa. "I can't read today, honey. I'm sorry."

"That's 'kay, we watch a wideo." The little one headed for the armoire and opened it, then installed a videotape all by himself. Brenda marveled at the boy's independence. Soon, Mickey Mouse was singing a happy tune and Daydan placed himself cozily at Brenda's side, snuggling into her with a wide grin.

"Dinner's almost ready, Brenda. We'll eat in the living room tonight. I'd rather you sit in a comfortable seat, 'cause I know your body hurts from the medicine." Katie appeared in a cutout area that led to the kitchen, wiping her hands on a kitchen towel.

There was a knock at the front door and Brenda found herself hoping it was Dr. Marcusson, even unconsciously retouching her hair at the possibility. Katie walked purposefully toward the entryway, removing her apron as she went.

"Wyatt!" Katie exclaimed, hugging the woman at the door while jumping excitedly. "You're back. How long are you staying?"

Wyatt. Slowly the name began to register upon Brenda's mind and she realized this was Luke's ex-fiancée. Brenda's eyes narrowed warily; an unconscious, but apparent expression of loathing crossed her face. Wyatt was short by Brenda's standards, probably about 5' 3" and plain. Her hair was long, desperately thin, and a natural mousy brown. She wore no makeup and a pair of loose-fitting army khakis with an ill-matching plaid shirt. She possessed a flawless, tanned complexion and full, bright-green eyes. Still, there was nothing spectacular about her. *What did he see in her?* Brenda wondered.

"Katie, I've missed you," Wyatt replied in a meek voice, reaching down to stroke Daydan's cheek. "I'm here as long as it takes to raise funds for next time. Barry's home tonight, his flight was late. He'll be speaking tomorrow at church, probably through glassy eyes."

Turning toward Brenda, Katie suddenly seemed to remember her. "I'm sorry, where are my manners?"

Brenda stood, partially facing the wall, as though she were invisible. Upon hearing the approaching introductions, she rotated and produced a counterfeit smile.

"Wyatt, this is Brenda Turner."

"Brenda, it's a pleasure to meet you." Wyatt reached out her hand and Brenda reluctantly reached for it, nodding as a response. "I'm actually here to see *you.*"

"Me?" Brenda hoped it wasn't true; she wanted nothing to do with this ninny.

Katie broke in, "Come on in, sit down, Wyatt."

Wyatt took Brenda's unwilling hand and led her back to the couch. "Brenda, I'm a nurse. I used to work for Dr. Marcusson." *So, that was what she called it.* "I know you have nystagmus and ataxia." She spoke quietly and, Brenda thought, condescendingly.

"What?" Brenda said curtly. She didn't have those things at all as far as she was concerned. And Miss Wyatt Ross could take her highfalutin words elsewhere.

"I'm sorry. Nystagmus is the double vision and eye problems you're having and ataxia is the dizziness."

"Yes." Brenda knew she was shooting daggers from her eyes, but she couldn't help it. Luke had been in love with this woman and no matter what the nurse had to say, Brenda hated her. "I can't read, you know." Brenda knew her tone sounded like that of a wounded cat, but found herself unable to be cordial. Jealousy coursed through her body. Unmerciful jealously for a man who had never given her more than his duty as a physician.

"Brenda, I think what Wyatt is trying to do is explain a few things about the disease for you," Katie intervened, trying to take the edge off Brenda's tone.

"What's to know? I have a disease, there are drugs to manage symptoms, end of story. When I can read about it, I will." Brenda began to walk toward the guest bedroom without excusing herself. Much to her surprise and dismay, Wyatt determinedly followed her and shut the door to the bedroom behind her.

"Brenda, I know this is frightening and you don't know me from Adam. But I'm a good friend of Dr. Marcusson's and I've had a lot of experience treating MS. At least let me explain some of the basics to prevent future attacks, okay?" Wyatt's tone was pleading. She placed the tapes on the desk near the bed and pulled on her hair nervously. "First of all, you need to keep your body cool. Heat only exacerbates your symptoms. No lingering baths or hot tubs. If you exercise, I'd recommend an air-conditioned gym, or swimming. You want to make sure you don't get to the point where you break a sweat."

"Then what's the point?" Brenda asked sarcastically.

Wyatt ignored the comment, concentrating on her task. "Secondly, you need to keep yourself stress-free. Now I know you're in a very high-profile job, so you might want to consider taking another position that has fewer responsibilities or possibly shortening your hours at the office."

Oh, you'd love that wouldn't you? Brenda eyed her opponent suspiciously and challenged the nurse by her very expression. She could tell Wyatt was uncomfortable with her and she took pleasure in her uneasiness, pushing her farther away. "I have managed more at twenty-seven than most women accomplish in a lifetime. Do you think I'm going to give it all up for a stress-free life? I'm sick, not crazy. I've worked too hard."

"Brenda, I didn't mean to suggest you give up your life. I only meant. . ."

"Never mind. I'm really tired, but I guess you and your books know that. I'd like a nap before dinner. If you don't mind." Brenda held the door of her bedroom open and waited for Wyatt, who stood stunned, to leave the room.

"Brenda, I've left a tape player with some multiple sclerosis books on tape. Please listen when you get a chance. You may be able to keep from ever getting ill again and you won't have to worry about your job, okay?" Wyatt was visibly shaken by the encounter and picked up her purse from the bed and left quickly.

"Katie, I'm sorry I must hurry, but I've got to pick up Barry at the airport. I'll see you tomorrow at church."

Katie saw the tears in Wyatt's eyes and immediately knew the cause. "Brenda!" Katie lifted her arms up in exasperation.

"I didn't do anything, I just told her I needed a nap!" Brenda replied before shutting her door to end any further discussion.

six

Sunday morning came quickly. Luke would have preferred to remain leisurely in bed, but the early sun pulled him from his sleep at his normal hour. He staggered the few steps to the kitchenette in his studio apartment and poured himself a bowl of cornflakes, smelling the milk before pouring. It had been a while since he'd visited the grocery store. He would have to include that on his "things to do" list for his one day off.

After breakfast, he walked out to the attached garage and found his beat-up Pinto missing. In its place was a sleek, black BMW convertible. "Brenda's car. I totally forgot." He slapped himself on the forehead. Luke had transferred Brenda's chart to Dr. Wilhelm along with a written explanation to Brenda that his practice did not allow for her therapy.

After listening to Wyatt, he had decided that the househunting idea was only an excuse to be near Brenda, which could only bring heartbreak. But, there was the matter of the car. He would have to see her and, inwardly, he worried that his eyes would give his true feelings away. It had been a cowardly thing to do, transferring her charts without consulting her. Clearly, God was making him face up to his feeble actions. *Lord, give me strength.*

Behind the racy sports car was Luke's prized possession and sole extravagance: a $1,500 mountain bike. Wyatt and Barry had laughed unceasingly when he showed them the bike, telling him he was the only man they knew with a bike worth more than his car. The thought of the scene made him smile and Luke was anxious for his day of worship and recreation. He put on his bicycling shorts, covered them with loose-fitting khakis and a chambray shirt and strapped a picnic lunch of scraps to his bike. He rode the two miles to church and figured he would gather a few teens from the youth group to accompany him for his weekly mountainside ride following service.

❧

Katie was frantic after one night with Brenda in their home and shared her concerns with her husband, "Jacob, she can't stay here anymore. She's scared to death. Last night when the gunshots went off, she threw herself on the floor. She didn't sleep at all, I heard the television on all night. It's obvious it bothers her to be here. We can't just let her live in anxiety, she'll never get well." Katie beseeched her husband with the facts in their bedroom, while he dressed for church.

"Did you explain to her that gunshots go off every night at eleven. That it's just somebody fooling around?"

"Jacob, she's never heard a gunshot before. As far as Brenda was concerned, they were coming for her. She's not going to get any better if she fears for her life. We've got to respect her doubts; East Palo Alto is not for everyone."

"I realize that. I'm just concerned you haven't given her enough time to feel safe here."

"Jacob, how do you explain to someone that gunfire doesn't mean anything? That it's just a part of the night here. We've been here so long, we don't even realize how strange some things are anymore."

"You're right, Katie. But, I don't want you to abandon her when she needs us most. And you can't stay with *her* right now. What if child protective services comes by about our request to keep Daydan permanently? We've got to maintain as normal a routine as possible."

Katie's eyes widened suddenly. "I think I have an idea."

"I don't like the sound of that at all." Jacob swayed his head back and forth while he finished buckling his belt. Katie whispered something into her husband's ear and he sighed loudly. "I wouldn't get too attached to *that* idea, but I'll do my best."

❧

Luke relished the warm spring morning air in his face, partaking in his own worship, as he rode his bicycle toward church. The sky was the bluest of blue with only a hint of one tiny cloud that served as a strong contrast against the rich azure. He breathed deeply and the spice of eucalyptus trees and freshly cut grass filled his senses. He kept a leisurely pace to keep himself cool for service and found himself at the sanctuary before he was ready to relinquish his bicycle.

"Luke!" Barry Ross's balding head and generous frame came rambling toward him with burly arms outstretched. Luke grabbed his old schoolmate and hugged him fiercely. The shadows from the historic church provided a parklike setting and the men sat beneath a sweet-smelling jasmine vine, anxious to catch up on their latest news. "I suppose Wyatt told you we ran out of funding in Africa. She's in talking with the deaconesses about further support now." Barry shook his head in despair, "I tell you, Luke. Sometimes I have to wonder what God expects. He tells us to go to Africa, then it feels like we're on our own."

"I know what you mean. . ." Luke dropped his chiseled jawline, immersed in his own thoughts. "I feel like God is taunting me with this woman by showing me what I can never have."

"Wyatt told me about Brenda. I'm sorry for her, Luke, and you too, of course. I thought it was all over though. Wyatt said you'd transferred her case."

"Unfortunately, I still have her car. What did Wyatt think of her?" Luke asked eagerly, feeling like a high schooler. "I thought she might call and tell me last night, but I guess you two were busy at the airport."

"Actually, Luke, I know Wyatt would never want to hurt your feelings, but she's pretty concerned about your emotions over this woman. Says you're going to keep seeing her on a personal level." Barry's friendly gray eyes were warm and concerned.

"I told Wyatt I was going to have Brenda help me house hunt, but I think I have ulterior motives."

"Luke, when was the last time you went out on a date?"

"With a woman?" Luke laughed.

"Yes, with a woman. You're thirty-six years old. It's about time you started thinking about settling down. Maybe you're just lonely. Have you been to the singles' group here?"

"Barry, you know I hate that stuff. As soon as someone's mother hears I'm a doctor, they're sending out wedding invitations. If God wants me to have a wife, He'll bring me one."

"Right to your doorstep, huh?" Barry asked. "Maybe you could steal your best friend's girl."

Luke laughed at the reference to Wyatt and Barry's shaky start. "You and Wyatt were meant to be. She and I never loved each other that way. I want what you and Wyatt have, but I'm happy single if that's God's plan for my life. I'm just frustrated right now, but I'll get over it."

"That's the right attitude. I just wanted to know where you stood. Wyatt sounded pretty upset over her encounter with Brenda yesterday. I feel better knowing you're standing on solid ground."

"Did Wyatt mention what happened? I know Brenda's personality can be a little harsh, but it's all an act. She's really vulnerable and sweet inside; her business exterior is all a front. As a matter of fact, Katie says she listened to the gospel yesterday and didn't even roll her eyes." Luke heard himself and knew he was justifying Brenda's bad behavior. He wanted to believe she was the woman destined for him; the woman God had hand-chosen to marry him and live out the rest of his days, but if she didn't dedicate her life to Christ, she was not the one. Barry and Wyatt were only trying to reinforce that fact. "You're right, I'm not thinking clearly. Oh, and chalk me up for a 20 percent increase in my African mission support. Wouldn't want you two hanging around too long." The two men laughed and hit each other on the back roughly as they walked into the sanctuary.

❧

Brenda paced back and forth in the guest room like a caged animal. The bedroom was pleasantly decorated in a blue and white floral motif with cranberry red pillows accenting the bed. Brenda had to admit that Katie's home was homey, even if it was in the ghetto.

Katie entered suddenly. "Brenda, you've got to quit worrying about work." Katie carried a load of laundry in her hands and tossed it onto the bed.

"You could have gone to church, I wouldn't have wilted in two hours time," Brenda chastised.

"I know. I was more concerned about your fears about being in our fair city."

"Katie, I'm sorry. I don't mean to be ungrateful, but I don't understand why you live here. You're nothing like these people. They shoot their guns off for fun, for heaven's sake. Doesn't that concern you? If not for yourself, for Daydan? I mean if you have to have a Bible study here, can't you rent a place for a day or something? I know you and Jacob mean well, but you don't have to be martyrs."

"Actually, Jacob did rent a garage when he first came here. He commuted for nearly a year before he felt like his home in Palo Alto wasn't home anymore. *This* was his home and where he felt God calling him to be."

"I don't get that at all. He lived in *Palo Alto*. Do you know what people will pay to live there today? God should love you no matter where you live."

Katie sat down with Brenda on the bed amidst the pile of clean-smelling laundry. "God does love us no matter where we live, Brenda. I know this is hard for you to understand, but God makes His wishes known to His people. He wants us here and nothing makes us happier than fulfilling His will for our lives. If I didn't live here, I wouldn't have Daydan, and he's the best part of my life."

"Even if I did what God wanted, I would never live here," Brenda stated emphatically. "No offense, Katie, but this place is scary. Don't you notice all the bars on the windows? That is not the sign of a healthy neighborhood."

Katie laughed and nodded. "I suppose you're right about that. You know what? If you did commit your life to God and you honestly *couldn't* live here, God wouldn't require it from you. He gives us each special gifts and calls us accordingly, so don't let that deter you."

"Yeah, okay."

"Listen, the reason I came in here is to tell you I have an idea. I know you have the campaign files that Mike Wilcox is looking for, and I know you're not likely to part with them. I have a compromise for the sake of *all* our jobs. And if you're not up to it, you'd better tell me."

Brenda sat on the edge of her seat, exhilarated at the possibility of working again.

"I'm listening!"

"Tomorrow, rather than go in to the office, we'll just drive there. You can wait in the car while I get what we need and then we'll go to your house to work. I can dictate the copy and you can edit it out loud. How does that sound?"

"Like sheer heaven!" Brenda clapped her hands together like a child at a birthday party, tossing her blond hair happily.

"You are a strange woman, Brenda Turner." Katie's sweet smile broke through and Brenda felt immense fortune by having the support of the petite brunette who cared so deeply for people.

The statuesque executive stooped and hugged her small assistant tightly. "Thank you!"

"Now, wait a minute, that was the easy part. There's a condition."

"Name your price," Brenda said without thinking.

"First, you don't read anything after I leave your house, understood?"

"Agreed. What else?"

"I know you're uncomfortable here and I'm concerned that it will affect your health. Jacob is talking to Wyatt Ross as we speak, about becoming your personal nurse for the next two weeks. I know money is not an issue for you and she could really use the salary for her ministry in Africa. You'd be doing each other a favor; you each have what the other needs," Katie said enthusiastically.

Immediately Brenda began shaking her head. "No, Katie. You have no idea what you're asking of me. Anyone but her, please." Brenda thought of the sweet-tempered missionary that Luke once loved, and all rational thinking left her. She felt an envious loathing rise within her.

"I've never met anyone who didn't think Wyatt was the crown jewel of people. We're only talking about two weeks. Even the lamest of your secretaries has lasted that long, so I know you have it in you."

"You wouldn't understand. You get along with everyone," Brenda argued.

"It has to be her or I won't help you. Wyatt's mission works with thousands of sick and dying children every year." Katie shook her head defiantly. "No, it definitely has to be Wyatt. I never met anyone who didn't absolutely love her, and you will too if you just give her a chance."

Brenda knew Katie wouldn't give in. She was generally so easygoing, but when there was something she felt strongly about, there was no use disputing.

"Fine."

Katie broke into a winning grin and began folding her laundry.

❧

"Absolutely not, Jacob. She hates me!" Wyatt cried. "No, she hates me with a vengeance and I have no idea why." Barry and Luke stood still, unwilling witnesses to the ugly scene.

"Wyatt, are you sure you're not reading a little more into this situation?" Luke asked innocently.

"Honey, you might be overreacting just a little bit," Barry added gently.

"You men are all the same. You see a blond with shampoo-commercial hair and your brains go right out the window. You have no idea who she really is! It's all an act, can't you see? To us women, well, her charms are quite transparent. We see the truth," Wyatt cried. The men all looked at her quizzically. Noting her out-of-character behavior, she calmly added, "I'm sorry, but I *don't* want to work for her. Not for two weeks, not even for two minutes. I can't think of anything I'd want to do less."

Luke stepped forward, wearing his most humble and disarming smile. "Come on, Wyatt. If she hires a nurse, we don't know what kind of care she'll get. You love the Lord! And you've worked with so many MS patients, you know the disease. Besides, just think how many children this salary might save in Africa." Luke saw Wyatt's face soften and he knew he was getting somewhere. It was then that he threw the final punch. "Please, Wyatt. Do it for me."

Wyatt closed her eyes in defeat. "All right, Luke. I'll do it, for you," she whispered.

Barry hugged his wife with pride. "That's my girl!"

"Great," Jacob said quickly, not giving her a chance to change her mind. "You'll start tomorrow evening at six o'clock. Brenda'll be on her best behavior, I promise. Gotta run, Daydan's waiting in Sunday school," Jacob said happily.

Wyatt stood defeated while Barry and Luke both beamed. "Thank you, Wyatt. I know God's love will shine through you. I can't think of anyone I'd rather have share the gospel with her than you. Your life is a living example and it will mean a lot to her, you'll see." Luke had all the confidence in the world in his friend. He knew her gift of evangelism and her all-encompassing love for humanity. Luke simply wasn't willing to give up the idea that God had handpicked Brenda to be his future wife. He tried to take Barry's earlier words of caution to heart, but something about Brenda had gripped him and wouldn't let go.

"Luke, I hope you're right, but I'm afraid she's going to see the worst example of Christianity in me. I can't help it; something about her brings out the worst in me," Wyatt admitted.

Luke knew Brenda could be severe, but he had never seen such a violent reaction in Wyatt. She *always* saw the best in people. He honestly wondered what Brenda could have done to upset her so, but figured ignorance was probably best.

"We'll have prayer behind you, Wyatt. You'll do fine and remember, you're working for God, not Brenda Turner," Barry said with his bulky arm still tightly woven around his petite wife. "Join us for lunch, Luke?"

"No, thanks, I'm taking the youth group for a bike ride this afternoon. They've been calling me an old man lately, so I'm going to take them up Skyline today and show them who's old."

"Take it easy on them, okay?" Wyatt said sweetly.

"Of course I will." Luke winked at Barry.

❧

Brenda packed her bags, made her bed, and perched on the edge, ready for home. She was so anxious to return to her old routine that she wished it was Monday already instead of early Sunday afternoon. Working gave Brenda a purpose in life and with this dreaded disease hanging over her head, she needed more than ever before to feel valuable. She scuffed the toes of her shoes impatiently on the rich country-blue carpet and tapped her fingers on the old rolltop desk beside her.

Katie walked by the doorway with yet another load of laundry and noticed the antsy inmate waiting to pounce. "Brenda, I never would have told you about working tomorrow if I thought you wouldn't rest. You know what Dr. Marcusson said about getting some sleep. Anxiety isn't good for you."

"I'm resting. See, I'm just sitting here." Brenda looked up with innocent eyes.

"Why don't you listen to some of the tapes Wyatt made for you? I would think you'd be interested in staying healthy. The healthier you are, the more money you can make," Katie said flippantly.

The incentive worked and Brenda reached for the untouched cassettes. "You're right, Katie. That will chew up some time," Brenda said enthusiastically, and Katie rolled her eyes.

"The boys will be home soon, so I'm going to close your door so they don't interrupt you. Lie down and take it easy while you listen."

Brenda lay back against her pillow and clicked the recorder on. The first thing she noticed was Wyatt's voice. There was concern in it that Brenda couldn't quite describe; a gentleness that Brenda would never own. She knew Luke must have been attracted to that sweetness, something Brenda had tried to copy in the past, only to have her brusque personality come tumbling out shortly thereafter. She sighed loudly and began concentrating on the words rather than Wyatt's soft voice.

Brenda heard for the first time some of the many statistics that describe the average MS patient. It was as if they had hand-selected her for the disease. *Why didn't someone tell me I was a candidate for such a devastating illness?* Brenda made a checklist as she listened.

Then came a seemingly endless list of symptoms that accompany the disease and she was thrilled when she had only three of the top ten. This was one competition she was willing to lose. Wyatt's voice listed the courses that several MS patients had followed: One had recovered to nearly normal after each and every episode; another was confined to a wheelchair shortly after the second episode. The best and worst cases. Brenda took solace in the fact that her bout sounded most like the woman who had recovered fully. There was no guarantee of course, but the comparison gave Brenda hope.

After her lengthy recitation about the disease, Wyatt addressed Brenda personally. "Know that I will be praying for you and I know Luke is praying for you. I have all the faith in the world that you will fully recover. Remember, you'll be feeling the effects of the drugs as well as your symptoms, so take heart, it will get better. I promise."

Brenda didn't know what to make of the personal note or why it touched her. Wyatt said she would be praying for Brenda. Even after her own rude behavior toward the missionary, she knew by the sincere voice that Wyatt would make good on her promise. She saw Wyatt in a new light, but her heart still burned with insecurity over the woman who had shared a special part of Luke's life.

Brenda emerged from her room with a new attitude. She found her empty place at the dinner table and sat. "I'm so excited about getting back to work. I can finish the campaign by Wednesday, present it to corporate on Thursday, and pitch it to the client next Monday. Star Digital ought to be public within two months."

Katie took Brenda's plate and loaded it with meat, mashed potatoes, and steamed vegetables. "Brenda, I'm glad you're excited about getting back, but remember, your body will probably not hold up under your old schedule."

Brenda ate her steamed vegetables quickly, the adrenaline of impending work giving her speed. "I know, I know," she said with a mouthful of food. "But do you think Mike Wilcox has been taking it easy while I've been gone? I've been out of work for two days, four if you count the weekend. I can assure you he's done everything he could to undermine my authority in that time." Brenda swallowed, took a quick sip of water, and stabbed another bite of meat. She was famished from the medication and felt like she couldn't shovel the food in fast enough.

"Let me put this in perspective for you. You were *blind* yesterday!" Katie fairly yelled. "You've got at least six weeks of vacation stored up, months if you count your sabbatical. Relax!"

Jacob intervened with a calm voice, "Brenda, I think what Katie is trying to say is that Star Digital's initial stock offering is secondary to your health. If you have to give that dream up, God will replace it with something better. It may be difficult to see in the midst of the trial, but God always works for the best."

Brenda stared at him questioningly. "No offense, Jacob, but if God is out there, He rewards those who work hard, don't you think? You can see I've been rewarded quite well in my career and I don't think it was by chance, do you?" she challenged, her jaw discreetly chewing rapidly.

"No, Brenda, of course I don't. But you're looking at success through the eyes of the world. God doesn't see people as we see them. He sees them on the inside. Take Wyatt Ross for example. Wyatt was a successful nurse in the world-class Stanford neurology department when she got the call to go to Africa and treat the poorest of the poor. She left one of the most respected hospitals in the country for a mission where she must beg for funding. She has pleaded with every major pharmaceutical company worldwide to get the supplies she needs just so a few children will make it through the night. The world may not see her as successful, but I'll tell you what, I bet God does." Jacob lifted his voice for emphasis.

"You're comparing Lee Iacocca with Mother Teresa. It's

apples and oranges," Brenda said through a mouthful of potatoes. She felt her face flush red at the comparison between her and Wyatt.

"Point taken, and you're right. God does give each of us different gifts. That wasn't a good analogy. But my point still stands, God doesn't see success as the world sees it. Since we all have different personalities, we all have different struggles."

"I don't see success as a struggle," Brenda replied curtly.

"Maybe not, but you seem willing to sacrifice your health for it, so maybe it's a bigger struggle than you think." His words touched a nerve. Jacob smiled at her graciously and reached for the bowl of potatoes, changing the subject. "Would you like more potatoes?" he asked while passing the bowl to her.

"No thanks," Brenda replied sheepishly. *Why do all religious people seem to have such a problem with success?* Her own parents had always discouraged a career for her, but she had shown everyone. She had amassed investments that no one could take away from her.

seven

Brenda was dressed in a fitted, navy Chanel suit, complete with pumps, tapping her fingers nervously on the nearby desk. Katie had to dress Daydan, make the family lunches, then dress herself. Brenda thought she might faint from the wait.

"Okay, Brenda. It's seven-thirty, time to go," Katie called from the kitchen.

Brenda bolted up, bags in hand, then fell back onto the bed for not allowing her balance to catch up with her. Jacob took the suitcases. He led her outside and Katie met her in the car with a Balance bar. "We'll stop at a drive-thru and get you a mocha. I wouldn't want you to suffer from caffeine withdrawal symptoms. It's been nearly two days," Katie joked.

Jacob hugged Brenda good-bye graciously while she self-consciously patted him on the back. "You're always welcome," he said.

"Thank you, Jacob." Brenda buckled herself in and Katie started the car.

As they dropped Daydan at his grandmother's, the mischievous toddler hopped into the front seat and planted a kiss on Brenda's cheek. "I miss you, 'kay? You come my house again." Daydan nodded for recognition.

"I sure will, you little cutie. You take care of great-grandma today, okay?"

Again the boy nodded and ran up to the house. Brenda opened the window and a light breeze filled the car. She closed her eyes in peace until she felt someone looking at her. She opened her eyes wide and saw a large dark outline beside her. She sat stone-faced, blinking her eyes for assurance that she was seeing a burly African-American teenager standing next to the car. She dropped her hand, freezing in panic. If she rolled the window up, she would appear prejudiced and he might hurt her. If she left the window down, all he had to do was grab her. She quickly determined that he was too close for her to do anything. She produced an instant smile, hoping he might just go away. If he wanted money, she was prepared to give it without a struggle.

The brawny teen reached into the car and held a piece of paper in his hand. He wore a broad, inviting smile and spoke pleasantly. "Excuse me, Miss. Did you lose this paper? I think I saw it fly from your car."

"I—uh, thanks." Brenda reached frantically for the page, still concerned he had ulterior motives.

"No problem. You have a nice day, now." The teen waved his large hand and ran to join a group of kids who were waiting for the bus.

Brenda dropped her hand, closed her eyes, and exhaled deeply just as Katie returned to the car. Knowing Katie wouldn't understand her obvious prejudice toward the poor, Brenda kept the incident to herself. The women stopped at the nearest espresso drive-thru, and then continued on to Star Digital. Brenda sipped on her mocha to settle her anxious stomach.

"Brenda, stay in the car. If you start to think you can do better than me in there this morning, just think about what Mike has probably told the staff about your time off. It won't do you any good to go fumbling into your office, agreed?"

Brenda only nodded, wishing she could jump out of the car and get back to her desk. She could crank out the rest of her campaign tactics in less than a day. She swallowed her morning dose of oral steroids and fidgeted while she waited.

❧

It was after one o'clock when Luke finished in surgery. He scrubbed down and returned to his cuffed slacks and dress shirt for the office. After lunch in the cafeteria, he headed for the exit.

"Dr. Marcusson. . .yoo-hoo, Dr. Marcusson. . ." A high-pitched voice called to Luke from across the room. He recognized the voice and turned to wait for Eve Moore to catch up with him. Eve was a petite beauty who knew her way around the hospital halls. It was common knowledge that she had her sights set on marrying a doctor, and today Luke seemed to be the grand prize in the bachelor game.

"Nurse Moore, how nice to see you," he said.

"I heard you performed groundbreaking brain surgery this morning with Dr. Olgilvy. The whole department is just buzzing, I wanted to be the first to congratulate you. It's not just *anyone* he asks to assist him." Luke opened his mouth to speak, but Eve beat him to the punch. "I also saw you finally traded that heap of yours in for a real car. I never imagined you in a BMW and a *convertible* too. Why, you must be hiding a real tiger in there," she said flirtatiously, poking him in the ribs.

"Actually, the car belongs to my girlfriend. She's ill right now and I've been using her car." *I can't believe I said that outright lie.* Although Luke chastised himself, he had no intention of straightening out the truth.

"Girlfriend? You must support her in grand style to drive a car like that. If you ever get tired of her. . ." She dropped her chin, but kept her eyes on his.

Luke clenched his teeth to avoid a thoughtless response. "Actually, she bought it herself." *There, that's a true statement.* "Have a pleasant day."

Luke walked out into the bright blue sunlight that made living in California worth the trouble of traffic and high prices. He sniffed the clean, eucalyptus scent and crossed the street, entering his office by the back door. A quick glance through the reception window showed a waiting area full of patients. His nurse, LeAnne, greeted him with a pile of phone messages in her hand.

"Luke, Mr. Townsend has been trying to reach you this morning. His wife disappeared from the nursing home again. He says he's ready to increase her dosages now and wants to discuss it with you. The police have been looking for her, but it's been four hours now."

Luke took the written message from her, "Thank you, let me know if you hear anything further. I think we might need to look into a different care home for her, one that specializes in physically healthy Alzheimers' patients. I'll call him back shortly, just let me get caught up."

"Mr. Montgomery is in room two, his chart's on the door. You've got a full schedule today, so I'll do my best to keep it moving. You've got a long list of doctors calling to confer with you about the surgery this morning and I told them you'd get back to them after hours. Also, Baylor called about your clinical trials. They're interested in talking in detail and wanted to see you at next month's conference. And Dr. Wilhelm called about Brenda Turner."

"Is everything okay?" he asked anxiously.

"Yes, he just wants to confer on her dosages." She gave him a quizzical look in response to the intensity of his voice.

"Thanks, LeAnne. It's too bad there aren't two of you. If I had you at home, I might have fresh milk in the fridge."

She smiled. "I hear there's a few nurses vying for the honor."

"Get back to work," he teased. "Keep it up and I'm going to tell your husband you're gossiping again." She grinned even wider.

&

Katie pulled her car into the driveway of the picturesque Victorian and looked at her passenger seriously. "Brenda, I don't know an easy way to tell you this, so I am just going to blurt it out. I don't want you to stress and I've considered not telling you, but I can't do that either, so here goes: Mike Wilcox had human resources bypass the password on your computer. He stole the files you created for the newest set-top box products and he's been working on the campaign since Thursday." Brenda remained unfazed, flipping her long blond hair casually over her shoulder.

"Katie, Mike couldn't write his way out of a paper bag. He may be a good salesman, but he's a terrible marketer. Most of the staff hate him, so who would help him?" Thinking about her statement, she continued, "But I guess a fair number of them hate me too, huh?" She crinkled her nose.

Katie reluctantly nodded. "He's got four days on you,

Brenda, and you're still not 100 percent. Please let it go. It's not worth it. Your stock options are vested regardless of who pulls off the deal."

"I have managed this product since it's infancy. It has to be me! I've got twelve companies making an inferior knockoff and one week to sell these set-top boxes to the best satellite providers in the business. Then we'll get the credit, Katie! Star's stock will make us millionaires! Do you trust that success to Mike Wilcox? We're talking one week. It's now or never. Tell me you're with me," Brenda said with full confidence, her competitive nature reveling at the challenge.

"I don't want to be a millionaire if it means sacrificing your health. I'm not sure I want to be a millionaire at all," Katie argued. "Dr. Marcusson told me if you continued at this pace, your health would pay the price. He doesn't want that on his conscience and neither do I."

Brenda paused at the mention of Luke, but went on, "I'm going to do it with or without you. It will be ten times easier with your eyes, but I'll find a way regardless. Dr. Marcusson would do the same thing for his precious Baylor fellowship!" Brenda spat.

"Fine, I'm with you, but only because I'm worried about you."

They spent the day surrounded by data, charts, and outlines of their prospective company and its executives. They studied each aspect of the campaign with painstaking detail; the only breaks they took were when Brenda's eyes sent her to the restroom to battle an overwhelming wave of nausea. Katie kept her fed and rationed her antifatigue pills throughout the day. All in all, the patient seemed to be doing well, surviving on pure adrenaline.

❧

Wyatt Ross knocked at the door three times, each time more aggressively, before entering the hurricane of paperwork uninvited. The living room was strewn with a flurry of graphs and Wyatt followed the paper trail to a bedroom office down the hall. It took her a moment to pick a pathway into the room, where she found Brenda and Katie in the midst of an animated conversation on a tapestry sofa against the wall.

"What on earth is going on in here?" Wyatt asked.

"Wyatt, welcome to campaign headquarters. It's a shutout game and we're in the final innings," Katie said. The two women, punchy from the long day, laughed themselves into hysteria while Wyatt stood by, flustered by the surrounding chaos. The women continued to laugh, tears streaming down their faces, until Katie glanced at her watch. "Oh my! It's six. I gotta go."

She made a hasty exit after promising Brenda that she'd be back at seven the following morning. "Wyatt, I left prescription instructions on the counter. Don't give her any more caffeine or antifatigue stuff; she needs to sleep." Katie slammed the door and was gone.

&

Luke saw his last patient at eight in the evening. Mrs. Townsend, his runaway Alzheimer's patient, had been found at four in the afternoon, nine hours after disappearing. Luke had gone by to check on her condition, which delayed his other appointments. Knowing his cupboards were bare, Luke decided to treat himself to dinner away from the hospital cafeteria.

He ate at a nearby salad restaurant, deciding to return Brenda's car after he finished. He mulled over various explanations of why he'd transferred her case without consent and rehearsed them in his head. He knew he couldn't tell her the truth; it would make him appear weak and unmanly. *I can't control myself around you, so I had to give you back to an old man who can handle it.*

When he arrived at the perfectly manicured Victorian on Harding Street, he was glad to see Wyatt's rental car parked outside. She would provide a buffer for his plan.

Luke knocked quietly on the door in case Brenda was sleeping, and Wyatt answered immediately. A continuous, high-speed clicking sound came from the front bedroom and Wyatt motioned him in. "How are things going?" he asked.

Wyatt looked up at him with big, sorrowful eyes. "Fine. She hasn't said a word to me. She's in her office." Wyatt led him to Brenda's home office.

The young vice president of marketing sat behind a custom-designed, built-in cherry wood desk, typing frantically on an oversized computer. Luke shook his head, exasperated. "Ahem. I know that's not Miss Turner at the keyboard, because I specifically told her to stay away from the written word. And most certainly that would include the computer."

❧

Brenda turned and faced the man who sent her heart soaring. She grappled with the black, elastic pirate patch she was wearing to prevent double vision. Her stomach turned in exhilaration, and once again she sat speechless while she drank in his good looks. His straight features had been tanned slightly by the sun and the green flecks in the soft brown of his eyes shone in the dwindling evening light. His easy, light brown hair was again parted neatly to the side and his towering build made his words disappear from her head.

"Miss Turner, did you hear me? It looks like you're reading and I'm certain I shared my concerns with you about its possible ill effects."

"I. . .I'm on deadline and. . ." *Just shoot me now.* Brenda ached over her lack of words. She glared at Wyatt, who offered no support but simply turned and walked back to the living room.

"Brenda," Luke came toward her and kneeled beside her. She looked into his warm eyes and felt lost inside their intense gaze. He took her hand and she felt the familiar electricity pulse through her body. His deep voice was quiet and filled with sincerity. "I'm not trying to punish you. If you damage your eyes, they might never return to normal. Do you think I'm telling you this again and again for fun?"

Brenda wet her lips and answered slowly, "No, Doctor, but my future depends on this week, it's everything I've worked toward. I know it's bad timing, but it can't be helped. I'll be able to relax in one week. I'll go to Hawaii if you want, lie on the beach, whatever you say, just let me have this week."

"It's not up to me." She felt him squeeze her hand tighter as he moved closer, a look of genuine concern crossing his brow. "I don't have control over the disease, but in many ways, Brenda, you do. Do what I ask; it's for your own good."

Brenda became lost in his hazel eyes, ready to promise him anything. She wanted to take his hand and put it to her cheek, but campaign concerns broke the magical spell. "I. . .I can't. I'm sorry." Brenda pulled her hand away and turned toward the computer. She couldn't continue to look into those eyes and say no to him. If he persisted, she could never deny him and she cringed at the thought. That must have been how her mother ended up so dependent upon her father. *Besides, you see me as nothing more than a statistic, a case to get you to Baylor.*

Luke looked up and saw Wyatt standing once again in the doorway. He shook his head and walked sullenly toward the door.

"I've been trying for two hours. Your plea was more heart-felt, but certainly no more effective," Wyatt explained as they entered the living room. "Do you want a cup of coffee?"

"That sounds great."

"Have a seat. You look exhausted again. Brenda probably senses you're the proverbial pot calling the kettle black when you say stop working." Wyatt didn't look at him, concentrating instead on pouring the coffee.

"I know I'm working a lot. But I've had this incredible opportunity. I've been assisting on computer-aided neurological surgeries. Patients will come from around the globe to have it done. Do you think Baylor will be able to ignore that kind of experience?"

"Full-time research at Baylor would take you away from a lot of personal contact."

"I know, but it's what I always *planned* to do. They may be close to the cure for MS and I want to be a part of that. Not just helping a few patients with the available drugs, but creating new ones; perhaps even the antidote. This oncology surgery will put me on the map. They filmed the surgery today for teaching purposes, sent it to fifty different schools and hospitals around the world. My phone rang off the hook with surgeons wanting to confer. I'll be able to go anywhere," Luke uncharacteristically bragged.

"Help! I'm surrounded by twisted, workaholic addicts." Wyatt threw up her arms and ran for the kitchen.

෨

Brenda appeared in the hallway from her office, holding on for dear life while the world spun around her. Continuously staring at the computer had finally led to an equilibrium revolt and Brenda wasn't sure which way was up. She swayed like a willow in the wind and clutched the doorway to hold her steady. Luke heard her grasp for the wall and turned to face her.

Brenda tried to maintain her upright position, "Aha! You do use technology. And you gave me that line about not watching television. Your surgery was seen around the country because Star Digital compressed the pictures into data that could travel over phone lines. That's because *I* was able to perform my job two years ago. You see?" Brenda's face beamed before she nearly fell over from the vertigo. Luke ran to her side.

Afraid that if she reached for his hand she would be on the floor, she held her place. He must have sensed her trepidation because he pulled her toward him, gently embraced her waist, and brought her to the couch, where he sat next to her. *He is so gorgeous,* she thought while trying to focus on his chiseled, masculine features as they whirled before her. *Like a great painting,* she thought, *something about him demands attention.* A wave of anger shot through her because she was unable to see him clearly.

"Brenda, your car's in the driveway. Wyatt's going to drop me at home. I should have told you sooner, but I've transferred your case back to Dr. Wilhelm." He paused, but Brenda remained silent. "If that's a problem, I can recommend another neurologist that might better suit your needs. I know that some patients have a difficult time seeing the doctor that diagnoses them."

Brenda lifted her sharp chin defiantly, holding her tongue.

He's not here to check on me, he's here to discard me. My case might harm his chances for his beloved research career. "No problem at all, Dr. Wilhelm will be fine. I appreciate your personal attention," she said coldly while rising from the ivory silk sofa. "I really must get back to work. Congratulations on your surgery, Dr. Marcusson. It's very exciting to begin a new venture. I wish you the best of luck with it. I'm sure Baylor will be calling soon," she said airily.

Brenda walked slowly into her office, widening her stance to avoid walking into the wall. She settled into her ergonomically correct chair, dropped her face in her hands, and cried.

eight

Brenda worked straight through the night with only one short nap. She lay down shortly before dawn and wondered whether Wyatt minded that Luke had visited her. *Does she still love him?* Brenda suddenly remembered her own status. Even if Luke were available, he'd seen enough devastation by multiple sclerosis to know better than to get involved with someone who had it. Luke's future didn't involve her and it was time she faced facts.

Wyatt awoke around six and made coffee for the two of them. She came in wearing a dark blue terry cloth robe with a tray in her hands. "You haven't slept at all, have you?"

"A couple hours, maybe." Brenda paused for a moment. "Wyatt, do you mind if I ask something personal? You don't have to answer if it makes you uncomfortable."

"Go ahead. I've got nothing to hide," Wyatt shrugged. She was happy to have Brenda even speak to her.

"I know about you and Luke. Did you ask him to stop seeing me as his patient? Are you two getting back together?" Brenda wasn't coy. She played her cards freely at work and saw no reason to do it differently in her personal life. If Luke and Wyatt were together, she wanted to know. If that were the reason she was being forced from his life, she would understand. If it was the MS, there was little she could do about that.

"Brenda, I'm a married woman! For nearly ten years now. Luke and I had a puppy love thing in graduate school, that's all. My husband Barry is Luke's best friend. They went to medical school together at Stanford. I love Luke like a brother." Wyatt rambled off her excuses quickly, as though she were ashamed that Brenda would think such a thing.

Brenda flushed red. "Oh, Wyatt, I'm sorry."

"You didn't know I was married? What did you think this

ring meant?" Wyatt held up her left hand.

"I never noticed it and I probably would have assumed it was from Luke if I had," Brenda admitted. "It seems I've developed a childish schoolgirl crush."

"Brenda, you're Luke's patient," Wyatt reasoned.

"I know—I'm sick, I don't believe in God, and Luke's moving to Texas. Is there anything I've forgotten?" Brenda cried. Noting Wyatt's fearful, furrowed brow, Brenda continued. "Don't worry. Luke's never offered me anything more than his medical expertise. I haven't had much experience with men and I read his concern as romantic interest. That's why I was so mean to you; I was jealous. I'm sure you'll all have a good laugh over this." Brenda stood to leave the room, but she swayed back into her bed instead. Wyatt sat alongside her easily, like an old friend.

"Brenda, I don't know what to say. When I first met you I wondered what it must be like to have a face or figure like yours. It reminded me of yearning to be like my Barbie dolls all over again. I guess I was a bit jealous myself. So, what is it like to have men knocking down your door?" Wyatt grinned, taking the edge off the conversation.

Brenda's blond hair dropped in long straggles around her shoulders. "Wyatt, I wouldn't know. In case you didn't notice, I have this little problem with tact. I say what I think, usually before I've thought about it. Men don't seem to take to kindly to it, I don't exactly ooze warmth. Still, Luke took it all in stride. But I'm not just jealous of you because of Luke. With both you and Katie, I'm so envious of that gentle quality you seem to have. And I wondered, if God made *me* like that, soft and gentle, would I believe in Him too?"

"Brenda, Katie and I are just two examples of God's women. There are lots of women in His kingdom who are not gentle or servants by nature; they've got to work at it. God has a place for everyone in His church. It's not an exclusive club."

"That's what Katie says, but my mother always told me that no Christian man would marry a woman with such a mouth. That's all my parents ever wanted for me was to find the right husband. If they knew how successful I am now, they would still see me as a failure." Brenda used the back of her slender hand to wipe a tear away.

"Your mother probably wanted that for you because it made her so happy. Were your parents happy together?"

"I guess they were, but my mother was a doormat. She did whatever my father asked, waited on him hand and foot. I never wanted that! That's why I was so attracted to Luke, he was the first man that was interested in my *job*. The first one that seemed to understand my need to succeed. You saw last night, he asked me to quit working on the computer, but he never *forced* me. He allowed me to make my own choice. Now I know it's because he doesn't really care, since I'm not his concern anymore."

Wyatt smiled with warmth. "I'm going to confide something in you, because I think it's important for you to understand the kind of man Luke is. He's a Christian and the Bible tells him he is not to be involved with a nonbeliever. God calls it being unequally yoked. God is number one in Luke's life and he needs to be with someone who has that same commitment. Trust me, without it you'd both be very unhappy. It's not a reflection on you, Brenda. You weren't wrong about Luke. He did think of you as more than a patient. In fact, he thought you were the most beautiful woman he'd ever seen. He loves your free spirit and your commitment to success and your outlandish sense of humor in the midst of such a difficult trial. I'm telling you this because I want to you know that Luke is not abandoning you, he's doing what he must to follow God's will."

Brenda was more confused than ever. Luke wouldn't see her on a personal basis not because of another woman or his job change, but because she didn't have a relationship with a God she couldn't see. She was helpless in that situation and it seemed so unfair to her. Everyone told her it wasn't an exclusive club, but no one told her how to get into it. Katie had tried to pray with her, but there had to be more to it than that. Perhaps if she found out what this God wanted, there would be a chance for her and Luke.

She looked at Wyatt hopefully when Katie came bounding in. "Let's get to work."

"Katie, I'm exhausted, I'm going to bed. I left the slide graphics and logos on my desk, would you get them made this morning?" Brenda asked sweetly. "I'm done for today, come back tomorrow." Every part of her ached. She felt as if she had fallen asleep and someone had kicked her in every joint of her body.

"A day off?" Katie replied as Brenda closed the door to her bedroom. "What's with her? She's a little cheery, wouldn't you say?"

"I think she's making a concerted effort to be more pleasant," Wyatt answered.

"That oughta last about a minute. Tell Brenda I'll take care of these slides. She'll be worried when she wakes up and comes back to her senses. I'll be back in the morning and we'll practice her presentation. She could do it in her sleep; I've never met more of a natural. I've got an appointment about Daydan's adoption, anyway. See you tomorrow."

≥≈

Brenda woke from a hard sleep at 2:04, according to her alarm clock. The shades were pulled and she didn't have the slightest idea whether it was morning or afternoon. "Wyatt?"

The nurse appeared in the doorway. "Brenda, are you hungry?"

"I'm starving. I want prime rib and a diet Pepsi," Brenda laughed. She lifted her worn frame from the bed and immediately fell to the floor.

Wyatt came immediately, lifting her from the rose-colored area rug covering the hardwood floors. "You have to remember to get up slowly. Let your equilibrium catch up with you. I'll get you a bowl of soup. Sorry, but we don't have any prime rib on hand and with all that prednisone in your system, I don't think you need a heavy meal."

"The slides—did Katie take them?"

"She told me to tell you they're done. She'll be by tomorrow to help you practice. You know, it's obvious there's a very important piece of Thursday's presentation that you've forgotten," Wyatt said cryptically as she left the room.

Brenda quickly talked herself through her checklist. "No, I've got the demographics, the psychographics, the company principle information, the slogan, the campaign outline, and the best product in town. Everything."

Wyatt came back into the room with a cold, wet towel and wiped Brenda's brow, "It's not a fancy marketing component, it's the simple fact that you can't walk alone. How do you expect your CEO, or worse yet, your buyers to take you seriously when you walk like a drunk. Are you willing to walk with a cane?"

"Absolutely not. They find out I'm sick and it's over for me."

"Legally, they can't fire you, Brenda."

"Maybe not legally, but they can demote me to a job I can 'handle,' and put an end to my career like that." She snapped her long fingers.

"I can teach you to walk with your affliction. God didn't give you those big feet for nothing," Wyatt teased.

Laughing, Brenda answered, "My dad used to tell me to take my skis off in the house." She shrugged her shoulders as thinking of her father brought tears to her eyes. Everything brought tears to her eyes on these medications.

Wyatt took Brenda's hands and stood in front of her. "When it's really bad, you'll need a walker, you've got to face that. But if you take it easy and you're having a good day, we can teach you to walk without assistance. All you have to remember is that your brain is not sending the right message to you, so we're going to reprogram your legs. We're going to learn to overcome what your brain is telling you by reacting first, before you receive any message. Trust your feet, not your head. Let your feet feel for you. If one foot starts to lose the floor, use the other to guide you." Wyatt walked with Brenda for nearly two hours.

Brenda was feeling extremely confident by the end of the lesson. "Now, let's try it in heels. I think I can do it."

"No heels—you're going to wear flats. It's not worth risking it, Brenda. If you fall, you'll look ridiculous and your campaign's shot. Flats are in style and it's not like you need the height." Wyatt craned her neck to look into Brenda's eyes.

"I don't even own flats. I like towering over people, especially little weaselly men like Mike Wilcox," Brenda smirked.

"You take far too much pleasure in that man's pain. Go get your sneakers, we're going to the mall. You can practice walking while you buy a pair of flat dress shoes. Brenda did as she was told and came running out of her bedroom, showing off her new skills. "Can we take my car? Please, please, please? I miss it so much and you'll look great driving it! Come on, I know you loved it last night when you took Luke home."

"What would the missionaries back home think?" she joked.

"Probably that you sold out in style!" Brenda had missed being outside and enjoyed the ride to the mall immensely, taking pained efforts to focus on the familiar drive. She lowered the top on her car at a stop sign and laughed aloud when Wyatt gave her a stern stare.

Once at the mall, Wyatt pulled a cane out of the trunk and handed it to Brenda.

"What do you expect me to do with it?"

"I want you to walk with it." Wyatt said enthusiastically.

"I don't want it. Put it back."

"Brenda! It's not just for you, it's so people around you know you need a little extra space."

"I'm not going in until you put it away. I'm not an invalid and I don't need that thing."

"You will be an invalid if you don't take care of yourself. You pull one more all-nighter and you'll find yourself needing more than this cane."

Brenda proceeded walking toward the store and relied on her ears to get her safely across the parking lot. Her eyes had indeed become worse since she had spent so much time on the computer, but she wasn't going to admit it. Brenda saw the curb coming up, but her leg didn't anticipate the height and she fell to the cement, stopping herself with her hands and forearms. She got up slowly so as not to anger her spinning brain and wiped the gravel from her scraped palms.

Wyatt made no mention of the incident and Brenda entered Bloomingdale's without further trouble. "Mommy's home, honey." She turned around for Wyatt's reaction and the two women laughed together, their earlier spat forgotten.

A bright white counter loomed, equipped with mirrors, cosmetics, and perfume. "Do you need makeup, Brenda?"

"Sit down, Wyatt. I'm giving you a makeover."

"A makeover? I don't think I'm the makeover type."

"Don't be ridiculous, with green eyes like that? And porcelain skin a model would die for? Your complexion is just so dry from the desert. Wouldn't you love to show up looking like a supermodel tonight for Barry?"

"Quite frankly, no."

"Come on, all men want their women to be glamorous once in a while. At least that's what the magazines say."

"The magazines that make their money off cosmetic ads."

"Now you're just being a stick in the mud. Sit down!" Brenda pushed her onto a chrome and white leather stool and proceeded to throw orders at the nearest salesgirl. "A light moisturizer, something she could wear on the plains of Africa." Brenda closed one eye and tried to concentrate on Wyatt's face.

"Are you going on a safari?" the salesgirl asked, intrigued.

"No, I'm a medical missionary in Kigali," Wyatt said brightly. Noticing Wyatt's old, ill-fitting khakis and ancient plaid shirt, the salesgirl pulled the makeup trays behind the counter.

"If you two just want to play dress-up, maybe you could go to Wal-Mart. Some of us have to work for a living."

Brenda's lighthearted mood snapped. "Excuse me! This woman is the wife of the prominent neurologist *Dr*. Barry Ross, and I am *vice president* of Star Digital. Well, missy, not only have you lost out on a nice commission, but I will be sending a letter to your manager, telling her of your unspeakable behavior. I don't think she'll be too pleased to know how you treat your customers."

"Brenda, please. . .it's okay, really," Wyatt said, trying to calm her down.

"No, it's not okay. This woman spends her day making frivolous women into Barbie dolls while you give up the life of luxury to help the poor. Who is she to make my friend feel like dirt? I won't stand for it!" Brenda was incensed and continued to berate the clerk, who apologized profusely.

Wyatt watched the whole thing as though in a trance. It took several moments before she regained her senses. "Brenda, please. Let me talk to you, please!" Wyatt pleaded and Brenda finally relented, following her across the aisle into the shoe department. "Brenda, that woman tried to hurt our feelings, but Jesus tells us to turn the other cheek."

"Turn the other cheek? Do you want to get walked over your entire life? That's ridiculous. Besides, Jesus didn't have to deal with snotty salesgirls."

"Brenda, that woman probably makes $6 an hour, $8 at best, in a town where the average home costs half a million dollars. She watches wealth displayed before her every day. She probably gets walked on day in and day out by rich socialites. Please give her a break, she's just trying to make a living. She only wants what you have, but has no idea how to go about it."

Brenda looked at the salesgirl and suddenly saw her as she herself had once been, desirous of a lifestyle that seemed only a dream. She now felt compassion where the anger had been. She nodded at Wyatt, using her assistance to get back to the counter. "Excuse me, I'm sorry I was rude. May we please try another shade of eye shadow?"

The clerk looked at the women warily, nodded, and brought the color palette out onto the counter. Brenda asked politely for each product she wished to try and purchased an entire skin care and color system for Wyatt. Wyatt begged her not to, but Brenda would have none of it. The two women paid for their purchases, selected some shoes, and walked to the car without a word.

Once inside the car, Brenda spoke. "I'm sorry I embarrassed you, Wyatt."

"Money is only temporary, Brenda. Right now, it may mean success, but it'll mean nothing in the end."

Brenda thought about Katie's earlier explanation of seeing people as God sees them and thought Wyatt must have perfected that ability. It was still something that eluded Brenda.

❧

"Brenda, I really wish you hadn't bought all these things. Now I'll feel positively compelled to use them. I might become downright vain!" Wyatt lifted their packages from the car and helped Brenda into the house.

"Don't be silly. I bought them as much for that salesgirl as I did for you. All that religious guilt my mother programmed into me. I never realized before how much differently. . .better. . .I'm treated because I have money. That situation just caused me to remember I never want to be without the power money brings. It only confirmed that I'll never live under other people's control again! I just get so frustrated with the poor that they don't try to better themselves. You know, get an education or a job with promotion opportunities. I think it's their own fault." Brenda tossed her blond locks unconsciously.

"When your father was alive, what did he do for a living?"

"He was an accountant. A very successful one, he worked a lot. Sometimes he didn't come home until after I'd gone to bed."

"So that explains part of your work ethic. Think about the child who has spent his life on welfare with only a mom to raise him. He's probably never seen anyone go to work. How does he learn what is expected behavior?"

"It's just the American way, everyone knows that," Brenda said without compassion.

"No, *you* know that. You've seen it put into action."

"I'm still mad at them for being poor, I can't help it. If they'd just do something about their situation, they wouldn't be that way."

Wyatt decided to emphasize the positive by changing the subject, "I was really proud of you with that gal today in Bloomingdale's. It took a lot of character to go back to that counter and apologize and even more to buy the makeup. You were a star today."

Brenda smiled widely, "I did do that, didn't I? Maybe some of your gentle nature is rubbing off on me. Do you think?" Brenda took pleasure in being able to humble herself for someone else.

"Brenda, I think God has special plans for you and I think He's working on them right now." Wyatt hugged her suddenly and Brenda self-consciously hugged back.

❧

Luke put off his hospital rounds until late afternoon. His patient load had been overwhelming with his newly added surgery and research schedule, and it kept him at the hospital continuously.

"Luke!" Dr. Olgilvy called from down the hall. Luke was surprised to be on a first-name basis after a mere six surgeries with the legendary oncologist. Frederick Ogilvy was a distinguished man of about fifty. He was still athletic for his age and not even winded after jogging to catch up with Luke. "The wife's having a dinner party. Just a small get-together with some of the area's cancer surgeons. You know the drill. Eight o'clock at my house. Here's the address. Is there a significant other?"

"No, just me." Luke took the calling card.

"Great, the wife'll get someone. You know how women are about an uneven number at the dinner table. Heaven forbid we dine with an odd number," Dr. Olgilvy said sarcastically while he slapped Luke on the back. "See you tonight."

Luke sighed outwardly, looking at the card in his hand. *Atherton. Of course, Dr. Olgilvy would live in Atherton, the most exclusive city on the Peninsula. What have I gotten myself into this time?* Luke wasn't comfortable in elite social circles and he cringed over situations like this.

It was 7:30 before Luke left the office and he was thankful that LeAnne had stayed late to sort out the many charts he had left in piles on his desk. "I'll be on the beeper, would you let the service know?"

Not waiting for an answer, Luke dashed out of the office and ran full speed to his Pinto for the short drive to his apartment. He dug deeply in his closet for the one suit he owned and selected a tie that was least likely to be outdated. He checked his reflection in the mirror and buttoned the double-breasted suit Wyatt had made him purchase for her wedding. It had been an expensive suit at the time and displayed Luke's tall, lean physique well. But now he wished he'd taken the time to improve his dress wardrobe. Certainly a doctor should own at least one fashionable suit.

He hopped into the Pinto and found himself wishing he'd kept Brenda's car one day longer. Before long he was on a shaded Atherton street, lushly canopied by the mature trees of the old money neighborhood. The mansion rooftops were barely discernible through the extensive greenery and iron gates. Luke located the address and turned onto a brick drive-way that wound for a short distance through the trees. In awe at the auspicious display of wealth, Luke found himself wishing that Brenda was by his side. "She would handle this like a pro and she'd let me know which fork to use," he said aloud.

A tuxedoed man met him at the end of the drive and motioned with his white-gloved hand to stop. "I'll take it from here, sir. Dr. and Mrs. Ogilvy are waiting." For the first time in his life, Luke winced at the sight of his battered vehicle. He had to give the hired valet credit though, not so much as a snicker crossed his face. He hoped there was a nice big tree to park the car behind.

The estate was a brick Tudor masterpiece that seemed to stretch on forever. Luke climbed several brick steps to a set of double glass doors. Another tuxedoed man answered. Luke couldn't avoid noticing that the help was dressed better than he was. The butler took his name and led him into a spacious living room, filled with half a dozen people. "Dr. Luke Marcusson," he announced. A small round of applause followed and Luke felt utterly out of place.

"Doctor, let me see those prizewinning hands I've heard so much about." The approaching redhead took his hands and examined them before her audience. "I'm Gloria Ogilvy. Such a pleasure to finally meet you." Luke guessed her to be about fifty, with flawless makeup and no wrinkles, whatsoever. Seeing Dr. Alto, a noted plastic surgeon, Luke guessed where they had gone. "Luke, I'm sure you know everyone. Dr. Alto and his wife, Miriam." Gloria Olgilvy pointed them out and Luke shook hands with each. "Dr. Wrightly and his wife, Jennifer; and I believe you're acquainted with Nurse Moore."

Eve Moore, the nurse with her eye on Luke, appeared from amid the small gathering. Gloria Olgilvy took each of their hands and melded them together in her own before letting go. "Don't they make an absolutely divine couple? My husband always says I have an eye for matchmaking."

Frederick Olgilvy piped in, "I never said any such ridiculous thing. Gentlemen, will you escort the ladies into the dining room? Dinner is served."

Luke offered his arm to Eve and smiled pleasantly. "Eve, you look very nice this evening." His tie felt tighter by the minute.

The dining room was a grand affair, swathed in ivory sheers that hung from the cathedral ceilings for an artistic, dramatic effect. The table, a great masterpiece of fine carved walnut was decorated for a feast. Tiny gold bowls filled with water were placed at each setting with a floating votive candle for atmospheric light.

Gold name cards sat atop gilded ivory plates. Luke held Eve's chair before finding his own beside her. She smiled easily, as though such luxury came naturally to her, and Luke found himself wondering whether Brenda would enjoy such a scene. *She would probably be forced to hold back her contagious giggle*.

As if reading his thoughts, Eve began the conversation. "So I noticed you had your old car back. Girlfriend feeling better, I hope? Or did you two have a little falling out?" she asked, batting her long eyelashes and looking at him from an angle with her chin dropped coquettishly.

The hostess overheard the conversation and barged right in. "Frederick, you told me he was single. I'm so sorry, Dr.

Marcusson, I hope I haven't placed you in an awkward position. No offense, of course, Eve; you're always welcome here." Luke looked at his dinner companion, wondering how often she'd been called upon to fill an empty seat for a bachelor doctor. He smiled and proceeded to answer Mrs. Olgilvy.

"No, not at all. Brenda's quite busy with a deadline." Luke felt his web of deception getting more tangled, but kept up the front easily after sensing a suspicious Eve Moore from the corner of his eye.

"What does she do? No, wait, let me guess. She's a surgical nurse," Gloria said loudly. The entire table erupted into polite laughter.

"Actually, she's not in the medical field. She's vice president of marketing for a technology company." Luke prayed silently over the bowl of lobster bisque that seemed to appear from nowhere. He began eating directly, hoping to divert the topic.

"How on earth did two such opposites attract?" Eve Moore probed.

"Pardon me?" Luke asked, hoping for a reprieve from the personal question he didn't have the answer for.

"You know women, old boy! She wants to know how you met," Dr. Olgilvy said. "Women are always so nosy," he mumbled, but his attention remained on Luke.

"We, uh, met at a conference on multiple sclerosis." *A very private conference,* he added silently.

"You won't have much time for those anymore. Not with a pair of skilled hands like yours," Dr. Alto said. "Frederick's got big plans for you."

"I'm not sure my future is in surgery, I'm partial to research," Luke admitted.

Luke had shocked the table and everyone stopped eating to look at him. Now more uneasy than ever, he felt like the centerpiece at the table and hoped the meal would end quickly so he could make a hasty exit. When a spring salad mix arrived with unrecognizable vegetables and a bitter taste, Luke knew his evening was only beginning.

Dr. Olgilvy sat and contemplated the comment during the

cessation of conversation. He crossed his arms and finally replied in a jovial tone, "Very noble of you, Luke. Very noble, indeed." The young doctor had only succeeded in impressing the famous surgeon. It was clear that Olgilvy still had plans for Luke, and the young doctor's own dreams were simply small obstacles to the wishes of the distinguished surgeon.

nine

Brenda left her shades open for the night and awakened to bright sunlight. *It's finally Thursday! And just look at that blue sky; it's got to be a sign for my presentation.*

Brenda started running a bath for herself. She found that she couldn't stand up in the shower, so she had learned to wash her blond locks in the sink before getting into her authentic antique claw-foot tub.

Brenda lathered quickly in the bath and used extreme caution by crawling out of the tub gingerly. The combination of hot water and her dizzy spells had sent her to the hard tile floor several times. She didn't want fresh bruises for her important appointment this morning.

She applied her makeup carefully, using her pirate patch loosely over one eye to do one side of her face and then shifting it to the other side. She blotted her lipstick with a tissue and emerged from the bathroom in her burgundy red tailored suit with dynamic gold buttons and opaque hose to hide her recent falls. "Well, how do I look?"

"Brenda, you look the picture of health. No one would ever guess," Wyatt answered truthfully.

"I know, and that's given me an idea. I'm going to take the cane with me today. If anyone has the nerve to ask, I'll just explain I had a little running incident or something. It's not worth breaking my neck to keep up appearances. Lots of people need canes for leg injuries and other things. It doesn't announce that I have multiple sclerosis."

"Just don't lie, Brenda. If you have to conceal the truth, that's fine. But please don't lie. God won't honor that."

"Very well, Wyatt. If it's important to you, I'll come up with something that isn't a lie." Brenda didn't know why Wyatt's opinion meant so much to her. After all, the two women had only known each other for a week. For some reason, however, it was important and she wouldn't break her promise. Brenda seemed to be growing a conscience with Wyatt around, and while it confused her, there was something about it that felt right.

Katie had taken Wednesday off in addition to the Tuesday Brenda had given her. It was so unlike her secretary to be off near an important deadline. Brenda knew there was something crucial happening in her home life, but to allow Katie her privacy, she hadn't asked for the details. In Katie's absence, Wyatt helped Brenda practice.

Katie opened the front door without knocking and had her hands full of iced mochas. "Caffeine all around. Get yours here!" Katie sounded happy, but her red face and swollen eyes told reality. She had tried to cover it with makeup, but had only succeeded in bringing more attention to its rosy puffiness.

"Katie?" Wyatt came forward, taking the drinks and setting them on the coffee table.

"No, please don't ask. Just be praying. Daydan's custody trial is Tuesday, our lawyer doesn't think we stand a chance, and that's all I can say without breaking into tears again, okay?"

Brenda and Wyatt nodded.

"We've got a big day ahead of us, Brenda. Let's just concentrate on the presentation. God will take care of us. God will take care of us," Katie said twice, as though trying to convince herself.

Brenda noticed that Katie was unsure of her statement and for once she felt like affirming the godly words. Katie had always seemed so confident in her faith, but today she seemed certain of nothing. It shook Brenda.

"Katie, go home. I can do this alone. I'm taking the cane, so I won't fall. I'll be fine." Brenda was wondering where her sudden concern for Katie came from; usually she only cared about what suited her, even if it was inconvenient for someone else.

"No, we're going to be millionaires, do you hear me?" Katie

said, trying to muster enthusiasm.

"I hear ya! Okay, Wyatt, say a prayer for us. It couldn't hurt," Brenda said breezily as they dashed out the door.

"I'll be on my knees," she promised.

za.

The beaming sunlight was too much too soon for an exhausted Luke. His patient load was wearing him thin. When he awoke, he grabbed his Bible from the nightstand and headed for breakfast at a nearby restaurant. It had been nearly two weeks since he'd been to a grocery store. He also took the newspaper to check out car ads. The Pinto had broken down on the way home from Dr. Olgilvy's dinner affair and that was the last straw. As a doctor, he had to have something more reliable.

Dr. Olgilvy had asked him to accompany him to Connecticut on Friday night to speak on their latest techniques at a weekend conference, so he didn't know when he could scrape the time to buy a car. Luke had arranged to have his patients seen by his partner, Dr. Byer, during his brief time away, but inwardly he worried about how long he could keep up this schedule. His research was beginning to fall behind. Two high-profile careers was one too many. A decision would have to made soon, but if Baylor didn't come through with an offer, the decision would be made for him.

Barry Ross was coming along to speak with some pharmaceutical companies at the conference about medications for his mission. Luke hoped that he and Barry would have a chance to talk.

za.

Brenda listened smugly while Mike Wilcox made his presentation. She took mental notes on his many mistakes and reformed her presentation in her mind to challenge each of his main points. She could tailor a presentation to fit anyone's needs at a moment's notice.

This was Mike's first audience with Star Digital's CEO and she almost felt sorry for him at how inept his concepts were. She watched CEO Dan White and he didn't seem to notice. It wouldn't become clear to him until Brenda spoke.

Mike finished and threw Brenda a condescending grin, as if to say, "Top that." She smiled broadly at him and stood before her company's executives, using her cane to lead her to the head of the conference table.

"Gentlemen, such a pleasure to see you this morning. As you can see by my cane, I've had a little trouble jogging lately, but I can assure you, you'll see me in the executive gym soon." The men laughed politely and she proceeded, changing into her business tone.

"Mr. Wilcox has a very good point about our product belonging in America's homes. Our set-top boxes are the best the satellite industry can provide for its customers. It allows the largest amount of choice to a consumer with the touch of a finger. However, we're a latecomer in the industry. What would make a satellite provider change its set-top box now? A cheaper, better alternative? Absolutely. Gentlemen, I have taken this opportunity to contract a field service team available for Day Graphics' use.

"The set-top boxes in today's market have a failure rate of forty percent. Yes, nearly half of all their present set-top boxes will fail in the field—in their customers' homes. And those numbers don't take into account the lack of field engineers able to fix the problem." Brenda pointed to her graphs to bolster her point, while the CEO nodded his head diligently. "Gentlemen, this should be Star Digital's new sales pitch." She unveiled her masterpiece and explained every detail in rapid succession.

When she was through, the men erupted into applause and came to congratulate her on a job well done. A job they knew would not go unnoticed by potential buyers. She saw Katie smiling proudly in the corner.

Brenda noticed Mike Wilcox angrily staring at her. "I know there's something wrong with you, *Miss* Turner! When I find out what you're hiding, and I will, there won't be a company in Silicon Valley that will even look at you. Then, the real vice president will stand up," he threatened.

Brenda mustered every bit of remaining strength and remained expressionless while she calmly replied, "Mr. Wilcox, I think we all know who the *real* vice president is. If you'd like to remain a product *manager,* I suggest you stick to your supporting role, where you belong." Brenda smiled condescendingly.

Katie took her hand and led her quickly to the car. Brenda took no satisfaction in her successful coup. For some reason, the same thrill she had always experienced with success was gone. "This stupid disease is removing the very life from me. I accomplished everything I planned today and I feel nothing! What's wrong?"

"Perhaps you're finding out that people are more important than money." Katie's voice cracked.

"I doubt it," Brenda grunted.

"Brenda Turner, I may lose my son on Tuesday. I'd give every cent of those millions to be able to raise him! Quit feeling sorry for yourself," Katie chastised.

Brenda sobered, thinking back to her own deceased parents. All the money in the world wouldn't allow her to tell them she was sorry. *Money may not be as important as people, but it sure can numb the pain,* she thought.

❧

Luke was happier than he'd been in a long time, being on research detail. As he sat down in the hospital cafeteria for lunch, he was almost disappointed to see Dr. Olgilvy coming toward him.

"Luke, my boy. You don't eat this slop too often, do you?"

"Enough to think it actually tastes pretty good," Luke replied facetiously.

"Oh, you *are* spending far too much time in here. Why don't you meet the wife and me at *Il Fornaio* this evening and bring your little vice president along. My wife is dying to see your taste in women. Just a casual little get-together where we can discuss the upcoming medical conference. What do you say? Gloria will keep your girlfriend busy while we talk business."

"I'd be honored, but I'm not sure about Brenda. She's been very busy at work. I don't even know if I could catch her," Luke lied, amazed at how much easier it was getting.

"Surely, that little filly carries a cell phone. Give her a call and we'll see you at seven tonight. I want you to be rested for our big trip to Connecticut tomorrow. I'm going to head downtown and get some real lunch. This stuff will rot your stomach."

Luke groaned. His lies were catching up with him, and now he was forced to produce a girlfriend that didn't exist. He thought about asking Wyatt to pose as Brenda, but quickly deserted the idea as more trouble. Besides, Wyatt would never support his lying, but Brenda might. Luke would have to tell Brenda the truth and pray that she'd go along with it. He regretted now that he had transferred her case.

He sauntered back to his office and sank into his chair. LeAnne brought in a stack of messages and patient charts that needed his signature. She looked at his defeated expression. "Why the long face?"

"If you only knew. LeAnne, would you get me Brenda Turner's number?"

"My favorite patient?" she said sarcastically.

"What is it about you women and Brenda Turner?" he called after her as she left his office.

She reappeared in the doorway a few seconds later with the number. "What a chauvinistic thing to say! You've been hanging around Olgilvy too long. But since you asked, I'll take great pleasure in telling you what *my* problem is with Brenda Turner. She's got the charm of a viper. Fortunately for her, it's wrapped in a blond, blue-eyed, supermodel package. I pity the man who enters her lair." LeAnne handed him the number with a wily grin.

Luke closed the door to his office and dialed the number three times before finally pushing the last digit. He felt like an awkward teenager calling his crush for the first time. She answered immediately, but groggily.

"Brenda? This is Luke Marcusson—the neurologist," he added nervously.

"I know who you are, Doctor."

"Did I wake you?" he asked gently.

"Unless you call at three A.M., you're likely to wake me. I do a lot of napping these days. Especially now that my deadline is complete until Monday when I make my presentation to our buyer. Wyatt's been helping me a lot with walking and keeping track of the plethora of pills you prescribed." *Brenda, you're doing it again.* Why she ran off at the mouth at every opportunity with Luke Marcusson was a complete mystery to her. "How is everything going with you and your new surgical career?" Brenda had missed the sound of his voice and wanted to hear him speak.

"That's actually what I'm calling about. I'm afraid I wasn't quite honest with you about my career change." Brenda thought about what Wyatt had told her about Luke being a man of integrity.

"Not honest? You?" she said softly.

"It's a long and detailed story, but it has to do with your car being in my possession. I told someone at work, stupidly, I might add, that it belonged to my girlfriend. I used your name and now I'm being asked to bring you to a private dinner party with the chief oncology surgeon. It's tonight and if you tell me no, I would hardly blame you. But, if you find it in your heart and you're not too tired, I would love to have you accompany me tonight. Frankly, it would save my hide with my new boss."

Brenda remained speechless. Was Luke Marcusson really asking her to pretend to be his girlfriend after he had dumped her as a patient? Her foolish pride told her to say no and let him handle his mess himself, but inwardly Brenda would give anything to be with Luke Marcusson, even for only a momentary charade.

"Brenda, are you still there?" Luke asked tentatively.

"Yes, I'm still here," Brenda whispered, still having trouble finding her voice.

"It was a stupid idea and I'm sorry I bothered you."

"Luke, no, don't hang up!" she cried desperately. "What time do I have to be ready and how would you like me to dress?" She sat up in her bed, throwing her rose coverlet to the side.

"Really? You'll do it? Brenda, I would be so grateful. Dr. Olgilvy is watching me closely and I don't want him to know I lied. I did it to save someone's feelings, but there's no excuse for it. Is 6:30 okay?"

"Only if you promise to take my car. I'm not sacrificing another pair of ten dollar nylons to that sock-eating Pinto of yours."

Luke laughed, "Listen, that Pinto—"

"I know, I know, Wyatt told me all about your loyalty to that car. It still owes me a pair of nylons!

"A nice dress, not too fancy, okay? And Brenda, I'm really looking forward to tonight."

"Me too, Doctor. Me too." They said good-bye and Brenda held the phone for a moment. Luke Marcusson had asked her out. Maybe it was only to help him in his ruse, but she was thankful for any opportunity to see him. After her long nap, Brenda's eyesight was really quite good. She could see clearly, although objects still seemed to spin relentlessly. She decided she would take the cane in the car with her, but use Luke for her crutch if he would allow it. That way, she would look like a doting girlfriend rather than an invalid.

Brenda stood slowly, but decided she was still too fatigued to get up. She called for Wyatt. "I'm sorry I didn't get the phone, Brenda. I was unloading groceries."

"That's fine, Wyatt. It was Luke Marcusson and I'm going to help him out on a business meeting tonight. Would you mind waking me up in an hour so I can get ready?"

"Sure, anything else I can do?" Wyatt asked with concern in her voice and Brenda knew the cause of it. She also knew that Luke probably wouldn't want his lie shared, especially with a pillar of righteousness like Wyatt.

Brenda looked down while she spoke, "I'm just helping him

out as a friend. Okay? You've been platonic friends for twelve years now, you said so yourself. That's all this is." Brenda cowered under her sheets, hoping to end the conversation.

"Luke *never* looked at me the way he looks at you, Brenda." Wyatt closed the door and Brenda was filled with elation by her last comment. *Does he look at me differently?* Brenda stared at the ceiling with a romantic, dreamy smile.

ten

Luke arrived promptly at 6:30. Wyatt gave him a wary look as she opened the large, white door.

"I know what you're going to say, Wyatt, and you can just save it. We're friends, I explained everything to her." He stepped in and sat on the plush ivory sofa.

Wyatt followed him, pointing her finger and whispering loudly, "Luke Matthew Marcusson, that woman has just been diagnosed with multiple sclerosis. Everything in her world has just changed. Games can get out of hand and innocent people get hurt. People that can't afford to be hurt! If this job is causing you to question your values, you better step back and question this job." Wyatt calmed her angry voice when she heard footsteps. Luke knew Wyatt to be a sweet and gentle soul, but when people she cared about were involved, she was as fierce as a mother bear protecting her cubs.

"Brenda?" Luke stood immediately, unprepared for what he saw. Brenda was an astonishing vision in a fitted deep navy dress, cut well above the knee to showcase her long, shapely legs. The tightly finished bodice was a scooped neckline with wraparound straps that bared her sexy, rounded shoulders, but kept her chest discreetly covered.

Her long blond hair flowed easily over her shoulders and the tropical blue of her eyes lit up against the navy backdrop of her dress. A simple strand of cultured pearls hung from her elegantly sculpted neck. Luke found himself wondering whether anyone would believe that this gorgeous woman was his girlfriend. "You look absolutely beautiful," he said breathily. It was all he could manage.

"Thank you, Luke. You look very nice yourself."

Wyatt interjected, "You can thank me for that. That suit was from my wedding. You two are a sight. Let me run and get my camera." Wyatt left the room and Luke searched for something to say.

"I can't thank you enough for doing this for me, Brenda. I should warn you that Mrs. Olgilvy tends to be a little nosy. Just so you know, I told her we met at an MS conference."

"Well, that slipped around the truth a bit. But I admire your creativity," Brenda giggled. Sharing in his charade made Brenda feel she had been let into his life. Not just his professional life, but his private life as well. She wanted to share in his triumphs and failures, she wanted to know more about who this strikingly good-looking man was inside.

"I didn't tell them about your MS. Of course, you can tell them if you like, but I wanted it to be your decision."

"Our friends are the only ones who know and I'd just as soon keep it that way. I don't want to be defined by a disease."

"That's fine," Luke agreed.

"I may need your help getting around in the restaurant. I don't do well in public situations. Too much activity for my eyes, you know? They don't know where to focus and I get confused easily. It was like that in the mall the other day. I think the neon lights bother me as well."

"I've heard that from some of my patients. A few of them have nicknamed it 'Wal-Mart syndrome' because it happens in stores with fluorescent lighting. I don't think you'll have to worry about that tonight. We going to *Il Fornaio* and it has soft, dim lights for atmosphere."

"I take a lot of clients there; I'll be right at home."

Wyatt reentered the room with a small Instamatic camera in her hand. "Move over here against the fireplace." She used her hand to wave them toward the back wall. "The marble will complement your navy attire perfectly. You two look like you went shopping together. Actually, you look like Barbie and Ken," she laughed.

Luke placed his arm around Brenda's slender waistline and the touch forced them to look into each other's eyes. The attraction was magnetic and Luke wondered whether he would ever pry his eyes from her. The spell was broken by Wyatt's abrupt cough. The two looked up and smiled eagerly for the camera. The hunger they felt for one another was painfully obvious. Luke kept his arm around Brenda's waist and led her to the door. She selected her cane from a brass umbrella holder near the door and folded it up, placing it in her clutch purse. Luke smiled at her obvious trust in him and vowed silently that he would never let her fall.

Wyatt followed them to the door and pulled Luke back at the last minute. "I'm warning you, Luke. Watch your step," she cautioned in a small, but threatening whisper.

❧

The buzz of whispered conversation increased in the trattoria as the radiant Brenda and imposing Luke entered the restaurant. Their height alone was enough to capture most people's fascination, but combined with their stunning good looks, eyes simply followed them. Frederick and Gloria Olgilvy stood when they entered, thrilled to be seen with the attractive couple.

Luke kept his arm protectively around Brenda's waist, as much to steady her balance as to establish ownership for all the gawking men. Brenda greeted Dr. and Mrs. Olgilvy with the utmost combination of friendliness and professionalism and Luke marveled at her allure all over again.

"Luke tells me you're very *personally* involved at the hospital, Mrs. Olgilvy," Brenda said smoothly. Luke laughed inwardly at her translation of Mrs. Olgilvy as a busybody.

"Well, I feel a certain responsibility for my husband's staff, you know, to see that they are fulfilled personally as well as professionally," Mrs. Olgilvy droned, completely taken in by Brenda. "I'm so glad Dr. Marcusson has found someone. I can't be everywhere, you know. And I do feel such a responsibility for my husband's staff," Gloria said.

Brenda gazed at Luke dreamily and stroked his arm, taking hold of his hand, sending shivers through his body, "I'm so relieved to know someone protects him from all those beautiful nurses." Brenda smiled easily and Luke had to look away to keep from laughing.

"My dear, you don't know how lucky you are to have such a

man. Professional, ethical, and I daresay he gives Mel Gibson a run for his money." Mrs. Olgilvy threw Luke a flirtatious grin.

"Enough of such frivolity. Luke tells me you're a vice president for a high-tech company. Which one?" Dr. Olgilvy asked.

"Star Digital, Dr. Olgilvy. We make set-top boxes for home entertainment satellite systems."

"Call me Frederick, please. Are you public yet?" he asked, obviously hoping for a stock tip.

Frederick? In all the years Luke had worked in the same hospital as Dr. Olgilvy, no one had ever been invited to address him as Frederick. Dr. Olgilvy hadn't even mentioned the upcoming medical conference and, somehow, Luke doubted he would.

"We're not public yet, but that may change soon," Brenda said with a smile.

She made polite and endearing small talk throughout the entire meal. She ate daintily, but managed to polish off a Caesar salad, a plate of *Penne Al Forno,* and tiramisu for dessert, without an obvious break in the conversation. Truly, she had elevated her wiles to an art form, and Luke was beginning to understand why perceptive women despised her. Luke didn't see her as deceitful, though; he saw her as a beautiful chameleon able to change colors for her particular audience. He was fascinated by her, but relished the thought of being alone with her later to have the *real* Brenda Turner return. The Brenda who would giggle endlessly over their triumph, the woman who fought her chronic illness with dignity and style. Ignoring the MS when possible and accommodating it when necessary.

After dinner, Luke escorted Brenda to the car slowly, careful to let her overworked eyes and equilibrium adjust. They had left after the Olgilvys so that Brenda could wobble out of the restaurant without being noticed. Luke was enraptured by the return of the natural, fun-loving Brenda that relished every moment of their game.

"I enjoyed the dinner, thank you so much for inviting me.

Dr. and Mrs. Olgilvy are quite charming. I think you were a little hard on her. Her heart's in the right place." Brenda laughed lightheartedly and Luke listened with pleasure.

"Tell me she's not annoying after she sets *you* up on a date!"

"Now why would she do that? Apparently, I already have the most eligible, handsome brain surgeon at Stanford," Brenda teased. "By the way, I hope you didn't have your eye on any cute nurses. I daresay Mrs. Olgilvy will be watching out for me."

Luke couldn't take it anymore. He stopped in his tracks along the populated University Avenue and pulled Brenda into his arms, searching the tropical blue of her eyes. "Brenda, a man can only take so much temptation." He drew her closer still and kissed her deliberately, his desire overwhelming him. He felt her kiss him back and he embraced her tighter still, closing his hand firmly around the back of her long, elegant neck. The two became lost in the moment, kissing each other freely, unconcerned with the bustling life around them. Luke ran his hands through her silky long hair, engaging the nape of her neck with both hands to keep her locked in his fiery embrace.

A passing car honked and Luke suddenly realized where he was and who he was with. He separated immediately, getting a hold on his consuming desire. "Brenda, I shouldn't have. I–I don't know what to say." Luke watched her blush and look away under the golden streetlight and knew he'd said the wrong thing. Of course he wanted to kiss her. Of course he knew what he was doing. Of course he wanted more. *More lies.*

"No, it's quite all right, Luke. Apparently, we got a little caught up in our one-act play. Let's just get home, shall we?" Luke recognized her standard cold response, the way she acted when hurt. He remembered it from when he had transferred her case. He wanted to hit himself for being the one to lose control. Wyatt had warned him. God had used Wyatt and Barry to warn him, but he hadn't heeded. Inwardly, he'd always known he wouldn't be able to handle the temptation of Brenda Turner.

Now that he had traveled too far down his dark path, he would have to desert her, for her own sake as well as his own.

God had commanded that a couple not be unequally yoked, but for the first time, Luke had questions. His passion spoke with a deafening fanfare, while God's voice seemed but a whisper.

❧

Brenda banished the simple front-step good-night from her memory and concentrated on the earlier passion of Luke's kiss. His memory filled her with warmth and she knew that *this* was the man for her. Surely, his God would never keep two such compatible people apart. What kind of God would do that? She lay awake in bed and contemplated the thought. Her body ached from MS exhaustion and pain, but her mind was filled with pleasure. She closed her eyes, unable to believe that she, such an active, athletic woman only two weeks ago, would be worn-out from a simple dinner.

She heard the front door shut and knew that Wyatt must finally be home. The nurse came to check on her and found her dreamily lying awake next to the soft light of a single, rose-scented candle.

"Brenda, did you have fun?" she asked cautiously.

"We had a wonderful time, Wyatt. He was an absolute gentlemen and he kept a tight hold on me. I looked the picture of health. He was charming and handsome and attentive. . .and he kissed me. He kissed me like I've never been kissed before. It was seductive and sweet and romantic and exhausting. I've never felt this way about a man before." She looked up at Wyatt, whose face was ghostly white. "I know how you feel about the religious thing, but God wouldn't want to deny our happiness. I know He wouldn't." Brenda smiled happily. "I think I love him. I know that's naive, I hardly know him, but I feel like I've known him forever."

Wyatt sighed loudly and somberly sat down on the edge of the bed. "Brenda, you're right, God wouldn't want to deny His people happiness. And that's why He's set up rules for us to live by. Just because something *feels* right doesn't mean it is.

The most important thing to Luke is God, Brenda. You will never be number one. Will you be able to deal with that? Being second to a God you don't believe is really there? I know you don't have much experience with men. I want you to understand that as women, we tend to be more emotional, letting our feelings run away with us. Many times, men let their emotions run away as well, in the name of sexual desire. Brenda, I'm not trying to say Luke's kiss didn't mean anything, I'm just trying to prepare you, in case he ends it. Remember, he's got his heart set on that job at Baylor."

"Wyatt, don't look at me that way with pity in your eyes. Luke *wants* to be with me. I know he does. I know by his kiss. I may not be very experienced with men, but this goes beyond experience. It's something I feel in the deepest part of my heart."

"I'm not saying he doesn't *want* to be with you. I'm just saying it wouldn't work out. Without a spiritual compatibility to build on, there's no basis for a relationship. Luke knows that. And when he thinks about it, he'll come to his senses. Brenda, I know that sounds harsh, but you'd truly have a life of pain after the excitement of courtship wore off. Barry, Katie, Jacob and I—we're all just trying to protect you. We all love you, both of you."

"You're jealous, aren't you? You've always been Luke's confidante and you're afraid I'll get in the way, aren't you?" Brenda spat, tears streaking freely down her cheeks.

Wyatt clung tightly to Brenda's hand, "Brenda, I would never do anything to hurt you or Luke. I love you both and I would like nothing more than to see you come to know Jesus in a personal way. That's what God and Luke both want, too. Let me get something for you to read. Are your eyes doing okay?" Wyatt relinquished Brenda's hand and left the bedroom. She returned shortly with a small tract in her hand and, when Brenda refused to take it, she set it on the nightstand.

After the door was closed, Brenda threw the tract across the room and sobbed herself to sleep.

eleven

Luke packed his suit in a garment bag and wished he had time to go shopping. He hated to spend the money, but this would be the third time in a week that Dr. Olgilvy would see him in the same suit. In all Luke's tenure at Stanford, he'd never once worried about his appearance, but suddenly his suit was outdated and his car decrepit. This job was definitely forcing him to make some changes in his attitudes and Luke hoped it was for the better. *Certainly there's nothing wrong with a doctor owning a reliable car and a decent suit.* He zipped the garment bag and shaving kit and set everything by the door while he waited for Barry.

Luke took the quiet moment and knelt down to pray. He found himself begging forgiveness for his lying and the kiss he'd stolen from Brenda the previous night. Then he thought about her warmth and the curve of her body and found himself asking for forgiveness again in the middle of his prayer. *Lord, You know my thoughts. Please, Lord, let her accept You and become an acceptable wife for me. I don't want to think of the alternative, but Your will be done.*

The young surgeon got off his knees just as the doorbell rang. Barry Ross stood at the door, an unhappy frown crossing his full face. "Wyatt's mighty angry at you and I can't say I blame her." Barry's lumbering frame filled the doorway and he walked past Luke without shaking his hand.

"Nice to see you, too," Luke said dejectedly while he motioned toward the simple, beige couch that was centered in the colorless room. "Have a seat." No paintings graced the walls and the off-white carpeting and white walls provided a sense of blankness. The same way Luke felt. He started to explain, "I thought I could handle it. She would impress the Olgilvys and I would get rid of Nurse Moore and be off to

104

Baylor before anything came of it. It started out as a simple plan, but you've seen Brenda. It's not just her looks either, I'm not *that* shallow. In all my years of practice, I've never met anyone like her. It's her inner strength; the way she handles everything with such grace and ease. She makes me laugh and I want to know more about her. Every time I learn something new, I want to know more. Her appeal is captivating and infectious. You should have seen her with Olgilvy. That man didn't talk a word of medicine last night. He sat utterly entranced."

"Luke, I'm not blaming you for being attracted to her. I'm blaming you for allowing things to progress to a point where you're both going to get hurt. What happens when Wyatt and I leave? You and Katie are all Brenda has, Luke. Have you seen anyone else around since she was diagnosed? When you finally realize that Brenda does not share your salvation, who's left to pick up the pieces? Do you expect her to handle this alone?"

"I'm not going to abandon her, if that's what you're worried about."

"So that means you're not moving to Texas if Baylor calls?"

Luke knew he was caught. He hadn't thought it through. "I don't know. . .but I'm buying a house here. Brenda's right. I'm paying too much in taxes; so for now, I guess, I'm staying put. Brenda's going to help me house hunt," Luke offered.

"I thought you decided that wasn't a good idea," Barry challenged.

"Well, I changed my mind. I'm getting too old to live in this unadorned abyss. I still live like a college grunt instead of a practicing neurologist." Luke knew he was justifying his time with Brenda. He knew God wasn't condoning his actions, yet he couldn't leave her while she needed him. House hunting seemed the perfect ruse.

"You've got three days to exact a plan that makes sense and I hope you find your answer in prayer!" Barry paused and looked around. "What is up with this apartment? This place looks exactly like it did five years ago. Aren't there furniture stores around here?"

Luke looked around at his bare walls and his desertlike environment and laughed. Barry grimaced, "You're one of a kind, my friend. Maybe you ought to hang that expensive bike on the wall for decoration! Come on or we'll miss our flight."

❧

Brenda slept until noon, her tired body aching from her evening out to dinner. She tried to get up to make some coffee, but found herself unable to lift herself from the bed. Staring at the clock, she tried to make out the time, but her overworked eyes were like wild little boys on a play yard. She closed her eyes, willing the accompanying nausea to go away. She didn't even have the energy to yell for Wyatt, but thanked her lucky stars when the young nurse appeared.

"Last night too much for you?" Wyatt asked with concern, placing coffee on the marble-topped nightstand.

"Ooh, my aching head is swimming. I feel like there are bees buzzing in the back of my brain and my eyesight is gone again. Just jumping colors and I'm sick to my stomach. I just want this moving to stop. . .oh, please, just make it stop." Brenda clutched her temples and gripped her hair, pulling it in frustration.

"So, I take it you'll be staying in today?"

Brenda's speech was slurred and her words slow, her symptoms were worse than ever. "I don't have a choice. It's too bad I don't drink alcohol, I could save a lot of money!"

"Someone seems to be forgetting a major presentation on Monday," Wyatt said, while trying to help her patient sit up. "The most important part of your career. Or was that just an exaggeration for my benefit?"

"No, I'm just resting so I'll be able to go through with it. I've learned a valuable lesson. I can't push my body like I used to. It just doesn't work that way. Instead of working overtime, it just shuts down and says no. Even my mouth feels like it's coming off novocaine. You know that feeling after the dentist? Oh, my whole head is buzzing." Brenda held her head in her hands and prayed that her head would stop spinning.

"Then we agree you're spending the day in bed." Wyatt lifted the floral coverlet over Brenda's shoulders and felt her head for a fever. This was no bug, it was all multiple sclerosis. Brenda had allowed her constant activity to further the intensity of her present bout with the disease.

Brenda moaned. "Trust me, you'll get no arguments from me." Motivated by the coffee sitting on the nightstand, she forced herself to sit up, but as she reached for the cup, her body slid sideways toward the center of the bed. Wyatt fluffed the pillows behind her and lifted Brenda to an upright position, but it was no use, she had lost her equilibrium. All she could manage was lying down. "You were right about overworking this body."

"The fewer exacerbations you have, the more likely you'll always fully recover. That's why we've been nagging you to slow down. Would you like to live with this permanently?"

Brenda grabbed her head again. "I don't want to live like this for one more minute!" she exclaimed. "Wyatt, what have I done? I can't beat this thing, this isn't some pushover client."

"You've got the whole weekend to recover. I'll go rent some movies and we'll *listen* to the classics until the weekend is over." Wyatt held Brenda and steadied her cup to give her a sip of coffee. "Here, take your medications."

"I can't drink any more until I visit the ladies' room," Brenda confessed. Wyatt helped her out of bed and Brenda sank to the floor on her hands and knees. "Don't mind me, it's just easier this way. I have more of an idea where the floor is." She laughed at her own appearance and proceeded on all fours to feel her way to the bathroom.

Wyatt called after her, through the closed door. "I think we should call Dr. Wilhelm about another corticosteroid run. You have an appointment this afternoon anyway."

Brenda's demeanor changed instantly and terror filled her voice. "No, Wyatt, not that. The pills are bad enough, I don't want to do another IV. Please, let me just see if I can sleep the damage off this weekend with the steroid pills. Change the appointment, I don't want to get dressed today. If I'm not better by Monday, I'll tell Dr. Wilhelm to go ahead." Brenda pleaded through the door.

"What about your presentation?" Wyatt asked, hoping to provide the necessary encouragement Brenda needed to fight her symptoms.

"Whatever happens, happens. I don't care."

"That statement elates me and worries me at the same time. Brenda? Talk to me." Wyatt rapped gently on the door.

Brenda opened the bathroom door and Wyatt adjusted her eyes to the floor where she came crawling out. "What's the difference? What use am I to anybody like this?"

"Listen to me. Depression is a big part of this disease and I see you sinking into it. You've got to live victoriously, do you understand? If you can't do it on your own, then I'm going to get you a prescription. I won't let this disease take your will."

"No more pills! I can't take it anymore. Pills to fight inflammation, pills to fight fatigue, pills to fight dizziness, pills to fight ulcers from all the medications, vitamins for the holistic route. No more! What good is a happy invalid? I *want* to wallow in it! Do you think Luke would want me if he could see me crawling to the toilet? I'm just one of his pathetic patients now. No neurologist is stupid enough to get involved with a disease he knows that well."

"Brenda, your life is not futile because you have multiple sclerosis. Luke knows you have MS, but that didn't stop him from thinking you were the one to impress Stanford's chief of neuro oncology."

"Do you think he'd still ask if he could see me today? And what about my CEO? Do you think he'd trust me? Entrust the future of Star Digital to a woman who can't stand on two feet. I'm useless like this and I *want* to be miserable, so leave me alone!" Brenda crawled into bed and pulled the cover over her head, hoping Wyatt would get the hint and leave, but she didn't.

"So you're just going to feel sorry for yourself?" Wyatt asked gently and without malice.

Brenda peeked out of the covers. "Yes, I have that right, you know. Not everything in this life is rainbows and gumdrops like you and Katie see it. I was perfectly healthy two weeks ago. Why shouldn't I feel sorry for myself? You have your health, a husband, and a life. I have this house and my job. And who knows what will happen now that I'm completely blinded by this stupid disease or now that I can't stand from dizziness. I may lose everything I have, so pardon my anger! Luke doesn't even think I'm good enough to be on his research project, much less in his life! He knows I'm not getting any better, doesn't he? It has nothing to do with your God!"

Wyatt's sweet demeanor took on a hard edge. "You may mock Katie and me for our optimism, but, Brenda, I've had children die in my arms from lack of money for a simple inoculation. Katie has had teens from her Bible study shot dead in the street and now she may lose her son to a system that doesn't care about that child! We're no strangers to suffering, Brenda, but I'll tell you what. My God is bigger than all the suffering in the world! You're just as diseased in your soul as from MS. And the sooner you wake up to that fact, the better off you'll be. I suppose life looks bleak right now, but if the worst thing that could happen to you is losing this house, consider yourself fortunate." Wyatt slammed the door and left Brenda wallowing in her self-pity and anger.

"That's supposed to make me feel better? Somebody's got it worse, so count my blessings! That's easy to say when you're standing up!" She shouted at the closed door, but her comment was answered only by the sound of the front door slamming. Suddenly, Brenda was alone and scared. *Wyatt wouldn't just leave without saying good-bye, would she?* Brenda allowed herself to give way to tears and soon she was sobbing hysterically, both for herself and the possible loss of her new friend.

She wanted to call Katie to come and stay with her in her present darkness, but there was no way she could find her phone number and dial it herself. Brenda just continued to cry. *They don't care about me anyway. If they did, I'd still be Luke's patient, not a reject he knows won't get him that promotion.*

He's just making Wyatt do his dirty work, so he can be through with it. I was right to vow never to get married. Men only complicate matters, I've got to concentrate on this sale at work and forget about Luke Marcusson.

❧

Wyatt slammed the front door of Luke's waiting area and several startled patients looked up at the commotion. She looked around and apologized, "I'm sorry, the door got away from me," she explained, but her frustration showed in her pained expression.

LeAnne came to the reception window and grinned. "Wyatt Ross, what a pleasure! But I'm afraid only Dr. Byer is in today. Luke isn't here. He's in Connecticut at a conference."

"I know, Barry's with him. I'm actually here to see if I can borrow a wheelchair."

"A wheelchair? Certainly. Do you know when you might be able to return it?"

"I'm not sure. If my patient continues to need one, I suppose we'll have to buy one. In the meantime, I'd rather not spend her money if it's not necessary. I'm leaving next week, so I suppose we'll do something about it before then."

"This isn't for Brenda Turner, is it?"

"Please don't get me started, LeAnne. It's been a very trying day and I'm struggling to understand God's will," Wyatt confessed.

"I'm sorry, Wyatt. Just a second and I'll get the wheelchair for you." LeAnne disappeared for a moment and reappeared with a silver wheelchair, an ancient relic that looked like it weighed a ton.

"I should have known Luke's wheelchairs would be prototypes," Wyatt joked, and LeAnne laughed out loud. "Well, I suppose it's better than nothing."

❧

Wyatt needed to cool down after her confrontation with Brenda and she allowed herself the luxury of lunch at her favorite salad bar. She bought a magazine and spent a relaxing afternoon walking around Stanford Shopping Center, the kind of expensive place she only afford to window-shop. It was after four before she returned to Brenda's home and found the patient in a hard sleep. Brenda finally awoke at five o'clock and was thrilled to hear Wyatt moving about in the kitchen. "Wyatt?"

She rushed to the room. "Brenda, how are you feeling?"

"Hungry. What else is new? They might as well give you a twenty-pound roast at the drugstore when you pick up these steroids. I just want to eat everything in sight."

"It'll get better. You won't be on those high doses forever. I called Dr. Wilhelm today. He wants me to keep a close eye on you in case your depression gets worse. He says you're probably still dealing with the reality of onset."

"Constant spinning, blinding darkness. That sounds a little depressing, doesn't it?"

Wyatt left the room and returned with the great, ugly wheelchair. "Get up, we're going out to dinner."

"I don't want to go out to dinner. I don't want people feeling sorry for me."

"Don't worry, where we're going no one's going to pity you. Get up or I'm leaving and you can find a new nurse," Wyatt threatened. Brenda was astounded at the show of force from such a normally meek character.

Convinced Wyatt was serious, Brenda pulled herself out of bed and crouched down to the floor. Wyatt pulled a pair of loose-fitting jeans from the closet and grabbed a company T-shirt from Brenda's drawer. Brenda felt the clothes. "I don't want to wear this."

"Get them on. . .now," Wyatt said, leaving no room for argument.

Brenda did as she was told and crawled out the front door. She watched the outline of Wyatt struggling with the heavy wheelchair down the front porch steps. Brenda gripped her way down the stairs and felt her way into the wheelchair. She brushed off her soiled knees, trying to salvage some semblance of pride.

Brenda fell asleep in the car and awoke as her BMW came to a stop. "Where are we?" she asked groggily.

"We're at the restaurant. Stay here until I get the wheelchair."

Brenda just nodded, hoping they were somewhere she could get a huge steak. While on the prednisone, Brenda had been craving red meat, something she hardly touched otherwise. Wyatt came around to the passenger side with the bulky chair and helped Brenda maintain her upright position while she got in. Wyatt then placed two pillow on each side of her. "These will keep you from slipping." Brenda looked up with innocently fearful eyes, but Wyatt was unmoved.

Brenda willed her eyes to focus on the single-story building in front of her. There was a line out the door and no other businesses around. Everything she saw was in fuzzy, outline form; there was no clarity in anything. They seemed to be in a industrial part of town, that was obvious by the oversized barrels stored behind cement fences. Wyatt parked the wheelchair behind the last person and slowly inched it forward as the gathering moved. "Where are we, some kind of buffet?" Brenda asked snobbishly.

"You might say that." Wyatt's tone gave nothing away and Brenda wondered when her beloved, sweet-hearted nurse would return. Or had she ruined this relationship too?

Brenda could hear the laughter and giggles of children. She heard people walk past her and say hello. She lifted her chin in greeting in case they were talking to her. Once inside the building, the lack of sun helped Brenda's eyesight and she finally concluded where Wyatt had taken her. "This is a soup kitchen!" she gasped.

"It's a Christian homeless shelter for families in transition," Wyatt corrected. "I suggest you keep your voice down so you don't offend anybody."

"Why on earth would you bring me here?"

"You told me the worst thing that could happen to you was that you might lose your house and your job. Well, here we are. These people have all been there. None of them has a home or a well-paying job. Do they look defeated?"

Brenda fought her eyes to focus, finally covering one to avoid the double vision. She saw smiling families sitting at the tables, praying over their meals, laughing at each others' jokes and enjoying the hearty meals in front of them.

"Most of these people trust the Lord and I can tell you, they are living victoriously. It may not look like it to you because you see them from the steps of a Victorian home in Palo Alto. But look closely at their faces. Do they *look* poor?"

Brenda was incensed; her body shook with anger that Wyatt would stoop so low. "So are we going to Bob Cratchett's house next to have a look at Tiny Tim? Maybe then, I'll repent and understand the evil of my ways."

"Brenda Turner, you are no better than these people. You *think* your money separates you from them, but God may take that wall away, so you might want to wipe that smug attitude from your personality," Wyatt said with an uncharacteristic sting in her voice.

A stout Mexican woman approached them with a tray in her hand. She bent over to look Brenda in the eye, reminding her she wasn't invisible. The Hispanic woman spoke in broken English, "I see you in chair. Very hard to get close to server, tables so tight, so I bring food." The woman placed the tray on a table and moved the regular chair from around a table to make room for Brenda. She then pushed Brenda's chair toward the plate. "If you need anything, yell for Yolanda."

There was nothing for Brenda to say but "thank you."

"You get used to system. Everybody friendly here, we trust Christ our Lord for His goodness. No worries." She said as she hobbled away with a limp. Wyatt followed after her and got a plate for herself before sitting across the table from Brenda.

"What has God done for these people? What do they possibly have to thank Him for?" Brenda was exasperated how people in such horrid conditions could praise a God they couldn't see for things He hadn't provided.

"They have a roof over their heads, food in their stomachs, and their families together. What more is there?"

"Life!" Brenda exclaimed.

"You mean a BMW, a stately home in the right neighborhood, that type of thing?'

"Yes, I guess I do. What's wrong with that?"

"Those things will all burn and the people that trusted in them along with it. The things these people are investing in, their God, their families, their assets are eternal. Your investments could be wiped out with the next big earthquake." Wyatt let the affront sink in for a moment, then added. "We're here, so enjoy. This is what God gave us today. Brenda, these people all have a thousand times what any of our patients in Africa have. God has blessed them richly."

Brenda ignored the God talk. If Wyatt wanted to belong to the God squad that was her choice, but Brenda knew better. She knew that relying on God was something that weak people did to give themselves comfort. So be it. She wasn't going to change Wyatt's mind. Wyatt had invested her whole life in believing in the invisible crutch, just like Brenda's own parents had done.

"This tastes great! What is it?" Brenda was shocked by the quality of the plate before her. She ravaged the meal, unable to control her ravenous appetite from the steroids.

"It's homemade tamales. The woman that runs the shelter is an expert Mexican chef," Wyatt replied.

Brenda was famished and finished her plate before Wyatt had even eaten one tamale. "Can I get more?" Brenda, though embarrassed, held up her empty plate. Who would have thought a homeless shelter would serve such an excellent meal? *No wonder these people don't bother looking for work.*

"I suppose you can have more now. The line is gone. That means anything remaining is free for seconds." Wyatt screeched her chair as she got up to get Brenda more, but before she left, Yolanda appeared with another plate of food.

"Thank you so much. How did you know?" Brenda stammered.

"You like my daughter. She skin and bones, but she eat like a horse."

Brenda laughed aloud and suddenly forgot where she was. She looked around her again and noticed no one was staring at her. When people had finished eating, they cleared their plates and stacked them on a corner table. Brenda was amazed by the organization of it all, like a well-oiled machine.

Following dinner Brenda motioned to Wyatt to come close. "If these people can follow this system so easily, why can't they follow society's system and keep a job?"

"In Silicon Valley? How many well-paying jobs do you think there are for uneducated, unskilled workers, most of whom have never learned the language."

"That's their fault. There must be fifty different trade schools in the area. Just about anyone could learn to be an electronics technician or computer repairman and English programs are a dime a dozen."

"What about tuition?"

"The government offers hundreds of grants. They're all over the Internet."

"Well, you're right. We'll just tell them when they're finished here at the homeless shelter, to run home and check their computer for the proper grants to get their education and when they're through with that, they can hire a nanny to watch their children while they get trained."

"Okay, I'll give you that, but anybody could get a job at a fast-food restaurant and Congress just upped the minimum wage, so where's the problem?"

"First of all, Brenda, five dollars an hour isn't going to support a family and secondly, all the minimum wage hike will do in most of these people's cases is reduce the number of hours employers can hire their workers. What's the first thing you ask on a application, Brenda? Where a person lives. What's the first thing you look at? Their appearance. Since these people don't have access to an address or proper interviewing attire, their prospects are nil. It's a big, negative cycle. Stop and look at the facts, Brenda. You think you have all the answers, but until you've walked a mile in their shoes, you have no idea what they face." Wyatt seemed personally offended by Brenda's belief system and the young executive could not understand it. It wasn't Wyatt she was talking about.

twelve

By Saturday morning at the medical conference, Luke was ready to clobber his fellow Stanford surgeon. Dr. Olgilvy had made a career living off his reputation and ultimately acted as though the entire neurological community should bow at his feet. Luke was expected to follow at a respectable distance and remain handy in case the proud doctor needed any support backing up his claims.

Luke had an hour before his next forum was scheduled to begin and he set about searching for Barry, a lunch companion he could stomach. He saw his distraught friend coming toward him and knew by the expression that Barry had not fared well with the pharmaceutical companies. "No luck?"

Barry shook his head in defeat. "They've got me figured out already. One sales rep told another until they all run when they see me coming. Sort of like you *working* doctors do to them."

"It'll happen. Let's go have lunch away from this ritzy hotel. Preferably someplace downtrodden that Frederick Olgilvy would never think to enter." Luke exited the hotel quickly, so as not to be noticed by Olgilvy.

They walked across the busy street to a diner named Fat's Place and sat down at the counter. An older waitress with jet black hair stood silent with her pad in expectation. Luke ordered a turkey on wheat with an iced tea and Barry ordered the meatloaf special and milk. The woman tore off a page and placed it on a wheel above the steel opening.

Luke lifted his tea toward Barry and cheered, "Here's to job misery!" The two glasses clinked and both men looked straight ahead into the steel kitchen. "So who's next on your pharmaceutical hit list?"

"I'm done for the day. Perhaps they'll be more generous on

Sunday," Barry said halfheartedly.

"I'll listen to a few pitches this afternoon and see if I have any luck. If they think it will get them closer to Olgilvy, we may have an advantage."

"That'd be great, I'm losing momentum. Besides, I promised Wyatt I'd look up Brenda's brother while I was here. He lives around here somewhere, and the ride will do me good. It'll give me something else to think about. Poor girl doesn't have any family out west."

"You're seeing Brenda's brother?"

Barry nodded. "Why?"

"I thought Brenda didn't want him to be bothered with her disease," Luke said. "She said he had enough to worry about with his family." He was astonished that Brenda would encourage such a visit. She always seemed so confident and self-assured about life on her own. He couldn't imagine her wanting someone to contact her family for her; it just didn't seem in her character.

"I'm not going to tell him about the MS, I'm just going to tell him Brenda wanted me to look him up. He can take it from there, if he chooses to."

"And *does* Brenda want you to look him up?" Luke asked warily.

"That's what Wyatt tells me. Although, something tells me I probably should have asked Brenda myself," Barry said doubtfully.

"Where Wyatt's concerned, that probably wouldn't have done you any good, anyway." They both laughed at Wyatt's gentle manner for getting what she wanted.

"Why don't you sit in on the forum this afternoon and I'll join you? I'd love to meet Brenda's brother," Luke suggested, anxious to know more about Brenda.

The two men finished their meals and left a sizable tip before crossing the street and entering the elegant hotel once again. Luke was accosted by Dr. Olgilvy as soon as he entered the lobby.

At Luke's afternoon forum, Dr. Olgilvy, truly a pioneer in

his field, engaged his audience of doctors. Luke began wondering whether this experience was worth working with the arrogant Dr. Olgilvy. *Perhaps Baylor will have called by the time I get back,* he hoped.

Luke snapped to attention when he heard his name. "And in conclusion, I would just like to extend my congratulations to Dr. Luke Marcusson, Stanford's new assistant chief surgeon in our neurosurgery department." Luke shot his head around to make sure he'd heard correctly. With everyone staring at him in the room, he knew he had. Olgilvy had given him the sought-after promotion in front of all of Luke's peers.

Luke didn't know whether to be elated at the boost to his career or infuriated that Olgilvy hadn't bothered to tell him beforehand. He just knew he wanted to escape and pretend he'd never heard it mentioned.

Luke stood up and went to the podium, shaking hands with the man he equally admired and despised. He tried to see him as God did, but try as he might, he was disgusted by his aggressive, tactless, grandstanding behavior. Would Baylor even consider him now that he was the "property" of Frederick Ogilvy? Luke prayed silently for God's peace and began, "I am deeply honored that my surgical skills have been recognized by such a talent in the field and I hope that our collaboration will eventually rid this world of fatal neurological tumors forever." Luke knew his speech was banal at best, but he was so thrown by Frederick's announcement, that he was at a loss for intelligent communication.

Their collaboration. In his short, ill-prepared address, he had accepted the position. Was there really a choice? He had been offered a dream position in front of his peers, any one of whom would have taken the job in a heartbeat. Declining would have been career suicide. Was God telling him to stay put or was Luke being corralled because of his own lies? Thinking back to Brenda's Oscar-winning performance and the steamy kiss they'd shared, Luke knew that this was his own doing.

Luke headed quickly toward Barry. "Follow me and act like we have somewhere to go. I need to escape." He and Barry smiled at well-wishers while jogging casually toward the exit. They soon dashed into a waiting yellow taxi at the curb.

"Where to?" the driver asked.

"Just drive, I'll have an address for you in a minute." Barry fumbled through his pockets and came up with the crumpled pink Post-It that Wyatt had given him. "It's 127 Briar Lane, in Kent."

Luke gazed at him inquisitively. "Where are we going?"

"Brenda's brother's. It'll get your mind off it. Besides, we have nearly an hour's drive. That'll keep you out of Olgilvy's path for the night, until you figure a way out of this mess."

"An hour's drive? Whoa, my friend. It would be a whole lot less expensive to rent a car. Hey, driver, pull over here, please."

The cab driver eased to the curb in front of the Hilton. After paying the fare for their three-block-long adventure, the two men stepped into the lobby of the hotel. Although they were not guests at this hotel, the concierge was able to make arrangements for a rental car, and within a half hour they were on the road to Kent.

"It's a good thing I brought my Visa card along," said Luke. I don't like to use it, but I carry it for emergencies like this." He steered the Ford Taurus onto the turnpike. "They didn't have any Pintos left, so I had to settle for this one," he joked, but Barry didn't laugh.

"Luke, there's something I need to say," Barry began soberly. "I've watched you change since you started working with Dr. Olgilvy and I don't like it. I never thought you enjoyed this job, and when you dressed Brenda up and paraded her in front of Olgilvy like some type of trophy, I knew you weren't thinking straight. This is a good job, Luke, but it needs to be right for you."

Luke nodded defeatedly.

"You're not arguing with me? Are you ill?" Barry asked.

"I miss my patients and the research. I've been so involved in their lives, involved in making advancements in their quality of life. I don't get the same satisfaction with the surgery. Of course, I love seeing them beat the cancer too, but just my hands are involved, not my heart. At least not the way it is with my neurology patients, who count on me so personally. Being there to have the same conversation every day with an Alzheimer's patient may sound routine, but the day their true personality comes back, there's nothing like it! It's why I became a doctor."

"There's the spark, Luke. Neurology is your answer."

"Do I have an answer? Do you think Olgilvy will accept my resignation without destroying my career? And what will leaving say to my peers? That I couldn't hack it, that's what. Quitting will make me a failure in neurology too. I've got no choice."

"I never thought about it, but I think you're right," Barry stated simply.

Luke rubbed his hand across his forehead. "Got any room in Africa?"

"Look at the bright side. You no longer have a huge decision dangling before you."

Luke kept his head bowed, trying to figure a way from the web he had tangled around himself.

Arriving in Kent before the evening sun had dropped, they approached a quaint New England farmhouse and knocked on the door. A teenage girl with a remarkable resemblance to Brenda answered the door, followed by her father.

Barry stammered, "We were looking for Doug and Kelly Turner." He looked again at the address on Post-It and compared it to the house number.

"I'm Doug Turner, and this is my daughter, Kaitlyn. How can I help you?"

Luke and Barry looked at one another in shock as if they had stepped into a time warp. "Again, Mr. Turner, I'm sorry. We were under the impression that your daughter was five. I'm Dr. Luke Marcusson and this is my associate, Dr. Barry Ross." Luke rarely attached his doctor status before his name, but he was hoping to add to their credibility to cover for their vast confusion. "We're friends of your sister Brenda and we were out here on business. We were hoping—" The door slammed in their face and the doctors gazed at one another in wonder.

The door quickly opened again and Doug Turner stepped out onto the porch. "Look gentlemen, I'm sorry to kill the messengers, but as far as I'm concerned, I don't have a sister."

"Your daughter looks remarkably like her aunt. Does Kaitlyn know about her?" Barry asked hopefully.

"Like I said, I don't have a sister and there's no sense dragging my children though the ugly scenes of the past."

"Your sister's ill," Luke offered as an olive branch, hoping to reach her brother's heart.

"Even if she were dying, there isn't a breathing relative who would attend her funeral," Doug replied curtly.

"Mr. Turner, I don't know what's happened in the past, but Brenda still has your daughter's picture on her mantle. She obviously cares."

"You know nothing about it. And if my sister was so concerned about her family ties, she'd know that Kaitlyn is now thirteen and stop living in the past. She'd know that Kaitlyn has two brothers, nine and eight. I wish you the best of luck with her, but she has no family as far as I'm concerned. Good evening." He stepped back inside the house, leaving Luke and Barry staring at each other on the front step.

"Apparently, Wyatt did not clear our visit with Brenda," Barry said as they walked back to the car.

"Apparently." The two men clambered into the car to begin the long drive back to the city. "I'm afraid Brenda's lack of friends extends to family as well." Luke looked at his hands set firmly on the wheel. How he ached for Brenda. Beautiful Brenda, without God, without her health, and without her family. Luke wished he could go to her and help crumble the cold exterior she used to protect herself, but he knew only God could do that.

Barry broke into his thoughts. "No wonder she's a workaholic."

❧

Sunday morning seemed as bleak to Brenda as the day before. The sunshine invaded the darkness of her closed eyes and she mourned the beautiful weather she couldn't see clearly. *Will I ever leave this wheelchair? Will I ever see Luke's handsome face clearly again?* Brenda's soft sobs began. Her face was red and her nose swollen from her many tears, but still they persisted unabated.

"Brenda, why don't you come to church with me this morning?" Wyatt's voice invaded the blindness but Brenda shook her head violently. "Come on, just to get out. No one will know you. What's the difference if they see you in a wheelchair?" She paused for a reaction. "I'll buy you breakfast afterward," she added.

"Hobee's?" came the meek but hopeful reply.

"Hobee's it is," Wyatt agreed.

Brenda crawled out of bed and over to her Georgian armoire across the room. She pulled out lingerie and crawled humbly to the bathroom with the unmentionables in her mouth.

"You're getting good at doing things yourself. I'm proud of you."

"Well, if you ever need a pet, I'm quite good at fetching things."

"I wouldn't take you. You eat too much. I'd be better off with a Great Dane," Wyatt cracked. Noticing the tears again, Wyatt immediately apologized, "Brenda, I was just trying to lighten your mood, honey. I'm sorry I hurt your feelings. You're in the depths of this bout, but you'll pull through, I know you will."

Brenda climbed to her feet, using the bed as a ladder and threw herself into Wyatt's arms, weeping with all her heart. "I hate this disease! What kind of disease takes away your abilities and self-respect within two weeks? Who ever heard of being so dizzy you need a wheelchair? If somebody told me that a month ago, I would have said they were crazy! I would have said they needed a psychologist, not a neurologist. I didn't even know what a neurologist did!" Brenda's deep, heart-wrenching sobs broke her sentences into syllables.

"Go ahead and cry." Wyatt felt her own tears coming on and the two women locked in a weepy embrace.

When Brenda felt better, she pulled away. "Wyatt, I'd give anything to have my health. I'd give my left arm if the room would only stop spinning and I might see life again. I worked so hard for all this furniture and the right wallpaper and it means nothing to me, nothing at all." They embraced again before Brenda slid to the floor and crawled into her closet, concentrating on finding clothes that matched.

"It's kind of hot for that blouse. Would you like me to pick something for you?" Wyatt offered.

"No. My arms look like I've been beaten from all my encounters with the walls. I think I'd be more comfortable in long sleeves." Brenda looked down while she spoke, her trademark confidence gone.

"If you're overheated that'll only make your symptoms worse. Please wear something without sleeves. Your arms are only bruised below the elbows. You can just keep your arms on the wheelchair, okay?" Wyatt was learning the art of negotiation.

Brenda nodded and allowed Wyatt to bring her a pale-pink silk tank top. She wore a pair of simple navy strap sandals and nodded when she was satisfied with her ensemble. Wyatt applied some powdered foundation and a pale berry lipstick for an added touch. "You look as beautiful as ever. The only difference is people will have to look down instead of up to see your lovely face. Now, you'll get to see how the short half lives." She relied on Wyatt for everything. The fear of her nurse leaving was growing. *What will I ever do without her?*

After Brenda's torrent of emotions, the women were late to church. Wyatt pushed Brenda's wheelchair into a darkened corner near the rear of the church. Brenda appreciated the anonymous seating and listened to the hymns with intensity, allowing the music of praise to fill her senses. Childhood memories invaded, but Brenda forced them back.

The pastor's sermon focused on unconfessed sin and Brenda felt she might explode from her own guilt. She imagined that everyone around her could see inside her and they *knew*. She thought of her mother and father and their tragic deaths. How she wished she could have made things right before they died. If only she'd put her foolish fears aside. Hot, stinging tears rolled down her cheeks uncontrolled.

The pastor's concluding words spoke with power to her, "Unconfessed sin is a living, breathing germ that breeds in our very soul, making us sicker and sicker until we can no longer function in our own carefully arranged world. If you have unconfessed sin in your life, or if you've never allowed Jesus to carry that burden for you, I urge you to come forward today and allow His blood to wash you clean. He can take it all away. Jesus came to save the lost, my friend. He loves you regardless of your past. Let Him free you. Come here and leave your cross at the altar of Christ."

Brenda felt her wheelchair move forward as if of its own volition. At first, just a few inches and then more. Her hands went to the silver guide wheel and she maneuvered the chair forward through the aisles, miraculously without so much as a bump into any obstacles. Once she neared the altar, she felt a warm hand placed on her shoulder. *What am I doing?* But as soon as the doubts rolled in, something dissipated them. Someone took control of her chair and she was wheeled slowly out of the sanctuary.

She heard a warm voice that told her how to pray for God's forgiveness and ask Jesus to come into her life. Brenda repeated the prayer, confessing silently. A warm peace washed over her and Brenda knew it was finished. She finally felt free. Free of the terrible, ravaging guilt that had plagued her for years. Brenda finished with a good, cleansing cry. Not the fearful, anxious tears that had plagued her for days, but a release of emotions that had been penned up inside her for years.

The same, gentle woman who had taught her to pray told her about a new believers' Bible study, gave her a Bible, and then pushed her back into the now quiet sanctuary. "Did you need to go somewhere?" she asked softly.

"No, Mary, I've got her." Wyatt's familiar voice filled Brenda's heart. If it hadn't been for Katie and Wyatt, Brenda would have never felt God's touch in her life. She knew that God's love had been shown through His people, unconditionally and consistently. It was as though He had given her a new family. When Brenda had nobody, they were there.

"Now I really owe you breakfast, huh?" Wyatt teased and both women laughed through their tears. They now shared a new bond that was stronger than the distance that would soon be between them.

Many church members stayed to offer Brenda their support in the upcoming months, offering her their congratulations for her new commitment. If she needed help reading her Bible or being driven somewhere, several women gave a name and offered a phone number. Outside the sanctuary, Wyatt placed the ancient wheelchair in the back seat of the convertible. When the summer season ended, Brenda would either have to invest in a smaller wheelchair or a car with a bigger trunk. In the meantime, Wyatt kept the top down and the wheelchair in the back.

"I feel like I could take on the world today. I feel free!" Brenda lifted her arms and let the breeze fill her senses. Wyatt placed her hands on Brenda's as she tore out of the church parking lot in the BMW. "You're beginning to like this car, aren't you?"

"I love it!" Wyatt surprisingly admitted.

"Wyatt Ross, you sound positively materialistic." Brenda laughed hysterically, while Wyatt wore a mischievous grin.

"It's ending soon. I'm going to enjoy the sporty life while God allows it."

"We'll enjoy it together! Let's drive to the beach after breakfast," Brenda said enthusiastically.

"I should have known you wouldn't go before food! What about your presentation tomorrow?" Wyatt asked cautiously.

"Forget it. Are we at Hobee's yet? I'm going to have a huge eggs Benedict with tons of hollandaise and a steaming cup of tea. I can taste it now."

"We better get you off those steroids soon or you won't be able to afford to feed yourself."

"You're buying today, remember?" Brenda said enthusiastically.

"I wouldn't have it any other way, Miss Turner. My new friend in Christ, you have so much excitement ahead of you. It won't be an easy transition, but it'll be the thrill-filled ride of your life."

"Doesn't God have an easy cruise version? I've had enough excitement for one year."

"I'm afraid not, so just sit back and enjoy the ride." Wyatt accelerated the BMW and Brenda relished the momentary rush.

※

Word spread quickly that Luke was Olgilvy's new assistant chief of neurosurgery. The promotion allowed him to get Barry the required medications for Africa. There wasn't a pharmaceuticals rep present who would turn down Olgilvy's new protégé. Dr. Ogilvy was flying on to Baltimore to consult at Johns Hopkins, so Luke and Barry were spared the ordeal of traveling back to California with him. Both men were exhausted by the events of the weekend, and they slept most of the way home on the red-eye flight. Luke arrived home to find an eviction notice in his mailbox. "These units are reserved for the exclusive use of physicians who are completing their residency at Stanford University Hospital," he read before crumpling the letter and throwing it across the room. He was exasperated. *Lord, what's next? First a new job, now a new house. What else?*

thirteen

Brenda nearly collapsed at the BMW following her big presentation for Day Graphics. She had given every ounce of
energy she had to the meeting, which she attended in her
wheelchair. It was abundantly clear that she would not be
able to work for some time. "Katie, in my briefcase are my
sabbatical papers. Would you see that they are turned in and
approved by the CEO? I'm going to take a vacation, spend
some time getting well."

"I'll see to it this afternoon, Brenda. You can't be fired now,"
Katie stated emphatically.

"Katie, of course I can. At my level, they call it corporate
downsizing. They'll say they're eliminating the position, hire
Mike Wilcox as corporate marketing manager instead of calling him a vice president and it's done. They do it every day.
Trust me, this is best. I'm going to need that initial public stock
offering money if I can't work for a while. A sabbatical will
take me through until we're public."

"Brenda, I hate to hear you talking like that. Have faith that
God will heal."

"He may, but I still need the break."

"I won't be in the office tomorrow; it's our court date." Katie
said the words without tears. Brenda thought she had probably
cried every last one she had for the possible loss of her son,
Daydan.

"Wyatt and I prayed for your family last night, Katie. I know
everything will work out. I just know it." Brenda had all the
confidence in the world that God would come through for the
Cummings family.

"How do you think we did in there?" Katie asked, ignoring
the subject of Daydan's court date.

"I think we'll be millionaires within the next year. They'd

have to be stupid to turn down our offer. We'll have our IPO and then we can both quit worrying about work for a while."

"Brenda, are you planning to leave Star Digital?"

"Not a chance, I'm just thinking about taking it easy for a while, that's all. Maybe allowing Mike Wilcox to take on some of the burden."

Katie shook her head. "I never thought I'd see the day."

Brenda arrived home without a care. Her obligations for work were over and now she could concentrate on beating her disease. She bought several books on the subject of multiple sclerosis, including a special diet book that worked for some. She had approached work with a full frontal attack and now she would do the same for her disease.

Katie assisted her up the porch steps. Once on the over-sized front verandah, Brenda slumped back into the chair. She thought she heard Luke's pleasant, low voice, and her heart skipped a beat at the mere possibility. She quickly opened the door.

Using the doorjamb to guide her, she stood up and took a half step into the house. Luke's voice raised in anger as soon as she stepped across the threshold. "Brenda Turner, why are you in the wheelchair? Why didn't you keep your appointment with Dr. Wilhelm? Do you have any regard for your health at all?" He chastised her without listening for answers.

Brenda's excitement about seeing him turned immediately to anger. "Dr. Marcusson, I told you the last time I saw you that I had a deadline. I'm not the kind of person who drops a major business deal just because I don't feel well. Would you let a patient suffer because you had a minor inconvenience at home?"

"That's a ridiculous analogy! You're coming with me for more corticosteroid therapy *now.*"

Brenda sat firmly back in her wheelchair and crossed her arms. "I'm not going anywhere. There are alternatives, you know. You doctors always want to pump us up with drugs." Brenda pointed to the armful of books that Katie was carrying to show the doctor what she meant.

"You want alternatives? Let me just give you the rundown of

your current choices: The vitamin route, which I understand Wyatt already started you on; there's bee sting therapy where some quack stings you twenty or so times for the bee venom; there's magnetic therapy, where you put magnets in your shoes; oxygen therapy, and an abundance of surefire cures readily available for purchase on the Internet. And you can try any one of them *after* you complete conventional therapy, which has a proven track record for bringing back your eyesight!" Luke came toward her.

"Luke, it's *my* treatment." Brenda used his first name, hoping to appeal to his emotions.

"There is no reason for you to be in a wheelchair right now. If you wanted to be in charge of your own health care, you should have thought about it during that work marathon that stressed your disease to this level." Luke gently tugged on her hands but she opposed him.

"Luke, you can't make me. . ."

"Wanna bet?" Luke swept her out of the chair and into his tightened, firm arms. "Wyatt, call the hospital and tell them we're on our way. Have them page Dr. Wilhelm. He struggled to control her long, flailing limbs and kicked the wheelchair away from them.

"My wheelchair!" she squealed.

"You won't be needing it." Luke remained calm, finally subduing her thrashing with his muscular arms.

"Luke, how do you know none of those alternative therapies work? You'd never believe in something unless it involved your paycheck!"

"Brenda, you're heartless sometimes. Like I said, you can try anything you like, *after* we get your eyesight back."

She had never heard him talk so intensely. Brenda was mere inches from his face and suddenly the memory of his powerful kiss filled her mind, completely eliminating her rising anger. His warm features subdued her temporarily. "I just want to be healthy," she said in a soft, vulnerable voice.

"Who do you think sees more MS patients cured, a neurologist or a traveling salesman? Have I ever given you reason not to trust me?" Luke opened the BMW and gently seated Brenda in the passenger seat. "Give me the keys."

"No," she declared.

"Give me the keys or we'll take the Pinto," Luke threatened and immediately Brenda tossed the keys, hearing the jingling stop as he caught them. The car started and Brenda knew she was destined for more IV steroids. *Oh, Lord, no.*

"Luke," she tried pleading. "This stuff makes me feel awful. At least when I'm on the pill form, I can manage some form of control in my life. I don't want to act like that again. I don't want to be out of control anymore. I've given my life to God. I don't want to be that monster again."

"Brenda, I heard about your conversion and no one could be happier for you." *Or me,* he thought. "But God uses medicine. All those alternatives are aimed at keeping you in remission. I'll even help you if that's what you want, but first you need to achieve remission. Besides, I have my own reasons for wanting your eyesight back. I'm getting kicked out of my campus housing. The complex is for medical residents only and I'm long past that stage. I've got a month to find a house. You said you'd help, but I doubt you'll be much good without your eyesight."

"Why don't you just hire a realtor?" she shot back.

"In *this* area?" he said lightly, using her own words. "Do you know what six percent of a $600,000 house is?"

The two laughed together and the present tension was broken. Brenda finally relented her will to Luke's, at least for the moment.

"Brenda, I'm not trying to control you, I'm trying to make you better in the best way I know how. If you won't see Dr. Wilhelm, I feel compelled to take over your treatment."

"I thought you didn't have time for me." Sadness enveloped her voice.

"Brenda, I lied to you. It was never that I didn't have time for you, although my schedule was beginning to squeeze out new patients. The real reason I transferred your case is. . ."

"I was too opinionated. I know, I've heard it before; it's the same reason I don't have friends. I'm trying! As a Christian, I am really trying to think of other people's feelings before I blast them with vicious opinions."

"Brenda, that has nothing to do with why I transferred your case."

She felt him looking at her and didn't know what to say. "I'm trying to be sweeter to people. If you put me on those high dosages of steroids, I know I won't be able to control myself. I want to be like Wyatt and Katie. Sweet and gentle, the kind of godly woman that people want to be around," she admitted openly.

At the next stoplight, Luke leaned over and looked directly into the sky blue eyes that couldn't return his gaze. "Brenda, God wants you to be the best possible Brenda you can be. He doesn't want another Katie or Wyatt. He wants us all to be servants, but that doesn't mean that you will serve in the same capacity. Do you understand?" Luke asked.

"No."

"Brenda, you have a combative personality. I'm sorry to say it that way, but you know it's true. Perhaps God wants you to be a lobbyist in Congress or fight for the poor to purchase housing. I'm not saying God wants you to be mean to people, but Brenda, He designed your skill set for your *own* ministry, not Katie's or Wyatt's. You have an incredible ability to handle confrontation. If you can do it lovingly, God will use that skill."

"Does that mean you'll take my case again?" Brenda asked.

"You never let me finish. I didn't transfer your case because I didn't like you. I transferred your case because if I looked into those incredible blue eyes to examine them one more time, I wouldn't have been able to control myself."

Brenda's face broke into a blushing smile while Luke raced toward the hospital.

fourteen

After two days on intravenous steroids, Brenda's eyesight was restored to the point that she could focus on everything around her. This time she vowed to stay away from all books, computers, and eyestrain until she was fully recovered. Luke visited her every day of her stay in the hospital, not as her doctor, but as her friend.

During her three-day stay, Luke and Wyatt brought their pastor in and anointed Brenda's head with oil, praying for healing. Brenda felt uncomfortable at first, with the many hands reaching for her and placing themselves on her head, but eventually, she sat back and relented to her new friends. Following the prayer, Brenda had Wyatt read the Scripture that ordained the anointing of oil and afterwards, she knew it was God's will.

"Brenda?" Luke entered her hospital room carrying a huge bouquet of pink tulips and yellow roses. "I didn't know what type of flowers you liked."

"Pink tulips and yellow roses are my exact favorites," she replied with a happy smile and a wink. "How did you know?"

"I see your eyesight is holding and you haven't lost your marketer's knack for saying the right thing. Dr. Wilhelm has released you; I'm here to take you home. I brought the real estate section. I thought I might read you a few entries. Are you up to it?"

"Since I won't be sleeping for a couple days, I say we give it a try. I don't feel nearly as achy this time." She paused a moment before adding humbly, "Thank you for forcing me to come. I'd like to return the favor; let's go house hunting." Luke signed Brenda's release papers and took her hand, lifting her from the wheelchair.

"Say good-bye to the wheelchair," Luke said.

Although she was able to see quite clearly, Brenda held firmly onto the muscular forearm of the handsome neurologist as he led her to the car. His touch warmed her heart and she took full advantage of the opportunity to be close.

"Your chariot awaits, madam." Luke swept his hand and opened the door to a brand-new, midnight-blue Toyota Camry.

"Luke! You didn't!" Brenda gasped incredulously.

"I did. Bought it yesterday. I thought it was kind of tacky to court you in your own car. Well, that, and the Pinto died on Highway 101 last Tuesday, leaving me little choice. I bought the blue because it complemented your eyes." Luke saw Brenda seated comfortably and headed for the driver's side.

Brenda waited for him to climb into the car. "I'm so proud of you. This was a big step!"

"I figured I'll have a new job, a new home. . .I might as well finish it off. Get rid of everything!"

"Not everything, I hope," Brenda said flirtatiously.

"No, not everything," Luke said softly, looking intently at Brenda. "At least until you find me a house!" Luke laughed and Brenda swatted his leg.

"Have you thought about what you want? A condo, town-home, house, mansion."

"Mansion?"

"Just seeing if you were paying attention. Do you want a yard? How many bedrooms?

"Okay, okay. One thing at a time. Yes, I want a yard and a house I can stay in forever. I don't want to have to move again, unless God takes me on a mission or elsewhere. Oh, and I only want one floor. I've seen too many patients have to leave their homes because they can't get up the stairs. I don't want that ever to be an issue."

Brenda looked at the solid, muscular man beside her and doubted that frailty would ever be a problem for Luke. He pushed a button and the sunroof peeled back, allowing rays of sunlight to shower on Brenda's golden blond hair. "Now, you're just showing off."

"I was trying to impress you."

"Consider me impressed." Brenda smiled, looking away in uncharacteristic shyness. This man made her feel like a silly schoolgirl. "What city did you have in mind?"

"Any suggestions?" Luke shrugged his shoulders. "I want something near the hospital."

"You'll pay for a Palo Alto address, but you'll never have to worry about resale value." Luke shot her a look. "Oh, that's right, you're not going anywhere. What about Menlo Park? It's close, the weather's perfect, and you can find a house as low as $250,000 or as high as over a million. Do you want to start there?"

"Menlo Park, yes. A million dollars, no," Luke answered.

"Okay, I have a few rules for my house hunting services. First, never act like you love a house. There is always something wrong with it! That attitude will help you in negotiations. You don't want to put the owners down, you just want to let the realtor know it's not exactly what you had in mind. It makes them work harder for the sale, thus lowering the price, but like I said with all the competition, you're still going to pay asking price."

"Is that all?"

"No. Secondly, don't get attached to a house until it's in escrow. That will save you unnecessary heartache when someone comes in and tops your offer."

"Deal. Is that it?"

"No, this is the most important part. No Eichlers, the flat-roofed houses."

"Okay, should I ask why?"

"Of course. Because they are seriously ugly, hard to sell, and I would have to question your taste."

"Okay, are those all the rules?"

"Yes."

"Then Menlo Park, here I come with the best looking non-real estate agent anywhere."

Brenda blushed red at the compliment. She wasn't used to receiving them and Luke seemed to offer them so easily. She thought it was one of his finest attributes.

~

Luke maneuvered his new sporty coupe quickly. He hadn't realized how much fun driving could be until he'd unloaded the Pinto. It was actually a pleasure instead of a constant prayer to get to his destination. Brenda's mood was gay and her health was extraordinary after her days on the intravenous steroids. Luke hoped the day wasn't too much for her; he glanced at her to make sure she was up to the task. *She is so beautiful, such perfect features. Lord, I can't thank you enough for calling her to Your kingdom.*

"Brenda, I've made a decision," Luke said, trying to keep her awake.

"Two in one week? You wouldn't be straining yourself, would you?" Brenda quipped. She knew how hard change was for Luke. She hoped her lighthearted treatment would help him move out of his comfort zone. At least long enough to get him a new home, something that was now a necessity after his eviction.

"Miss Turner, who's working for whom here?" he said lightly, his hazel-green eyes sparkling with mischief.

"That depends, we haven't discussed salary."

"Of course. Dinner at the restaurant of your choice?"

"Great. I want the Lodge."

"The steak place?" he asked skeptically.

"Yes, I want a big salad, a huge prime rib with tons of horseradish and I'll top it off with a mud pie. Doesn't that sound great?" Brenda's eyes were wide with anticipation and she rubbed her hands together in pleasure over the thought.

"I better find a house soon or I'll be too broke to buy it."

"You're the one who insisted I take the intravenous steroids. It's only fair you take on a few of my increased grocery bills. It's the least you can do."

~

Luke took a sharp right turn down a lush, oak-lined cul-de-sac. The houses were well-spaced with extensive, manicured front lawns that would be ideal for a pickup football game after Thanksgiving dinner. Spring flowers lined each long walkway and the house for sale had a mature sequoia tree that shaded the entire yard. The house was a remodeled rancher with several white French windows and an elongated set of double front doors that marked its dramatic entrance. "How much is this neighborhood?" Luke asked, knowing it was probably above his self-imposed price range.

"Just look at it first. The moths won't get out of your wallet if you just look. I promise," Brenda giggled under her breath.

"I am not cheap!" Luke exclaimed passionately.

She turned serious, "I know, Luke. You're very generous. However, I think you're looking at this house thing in the wrong light. You've got to realize a house is an investment. In your income bracket, you're probably paying forty percent in taxes right now. By sheltering some of that income in a house, you'll have more to spend where you want to spend it; missions, the church, wherever. Not sheltering income is bad stewardship."

"Bad stewardship. Where did you learn that?"

"Wyatt asked me where I thought I might have trouble with sin; you know, besides my temper. I told her with money, so she taught me about stewardship. You know the parable about the men who each receive money for investing? Each of them increases their boss's money, except the one who buried it. God has plans for your salary, Luke."

Exiting the car, they were greeted by a friendly real estate agent dressed in an ivory suit. The agent's dark bob and big brown eyes were highlighted by the light color she wore. Her impeccable, professional appearance caused Brenda to feel self-conscious in her simple jeans and short-sleeved sweater. She wished she'd gone home to change after leaving the hospital. The agent handed them an information sheet and Brenda stole it from Luke's hands before he could see the price.

"Just look at it first," she cautioned.

"I'm Jessie Morgan," The realtor said. "If you have any questions, please feel free to ask. Make yourselves at home. Are you two getting ready to start a family?" she asked innocently. Luke and Brenda looked at one another guiltily and both were at a loss for words. "I'm sorry. The reason I asked is that this house is perfect for a growing family. The house was redesigned casually, with children in mind. The backyard is completely self-contained with an included swing set. There are lots of preschoolers and infants on the block and you're in a wonderful school district here. It's part of the Menlo-Atherton district."

"Atherton? Brenda, we're. . ."

". . .in Menlo Park still and it doesn't cost anything to look," she whispered, pulling him away from the agent.

❧

Luke was captivated by the house, every last crevice. He loved the sunken living room, the cream carpet, the French doors, the oversized tub in the master bathroom, and especially the park-like backyard. He could just imagine playing baseball with his future sons under the great oak tree. There was a trickle of a running creek in the back as well as a basketball court and the swing set. Watching Brenda wander around the house, he imagined her entertaining their friends in her casual, take-charge manner. This is where he wanted to grow old with her. Catching her eye, he snapped out of his reverie and followed her into the kitchen.

Brenda clapped her hands together and ran toward him. Her eyes sparkled with excitement. "Luke, look at this kitchen. It's perfect! Look at these huge countertops and the country French cabinets with the plate racks. I couldn't have designed it better myself. These hardwood floors are just gorgeous!"

"What about not getting attached to a house before escrow? And what was all that stuff about there always being something wrong with a place?" Luke chided jokingly.

"Why do you think I told you all that? Because those are my weaknesses. I never can seem to control my emotions where the perfect home is concerned." She covered her mouth to contain a laugh.

He grimaced at her while shaking his head. "This is the perfect home, isn't it?"

She nodded. "This is it, Luke."

Luke knew it was the right home and that he wanted to take Brenda as his wife and move in the very next day, but he had to pray. This wasn't like him, he couldn't just purchase a house at the drop of a hat. He had to think about it, stew over it. He didn't even know what it cost. A new job, a new house, possibly a wife—it was all too much. "Thank you," he said to the realtor and raced out the door, pulling Brenda by the hand.

"Luke, what are you doing? Don't you want to talk to the realtor and maybe make an offer?"

"I can't work this way, Brenda. I have to pray about it. It's my home! You may go off and spend a wad of cash readily, but I don't!" he barked. Brenda broke away from his grip, an expression of pain coming crossing her face.

≈

Brenda was so hurt by Luke's uncharacteristic outburst that she feigned fatigue, rather than have to eat dinner with him. She couldn't go through an entire meal pretending, her medications would make that literally impossible. They made her so much more transparent and right now, she hated such a blatant side effect. Luke drove her home. He walked her to the door, but once she was safely on the porch, he turned and hurried back to his car. When Brenda entered the house she found Wyatt and Barry watching a movie on the couch. Wyatt was in tears with a wadded up tissue in her hand.

"Wyatt, what's the matter?" Brenda ran to her, looking at Barry suspiciously.

"Nothing, Brenda, it's this movie. It's so sad!" she wailed.

Brenda looked at the screen and saw they were watching *Jurassic Park*. "Wyatt, you're watching a movie about dinosaurs."

"I know," she wailed.

Barry grabbed the remote and flipped the television off. "I think that's enough television. What Wyatt's trying to tell you, Brenda, is that she's pregnant."

Wyatt broke into loud sob. "Can you believe it? We've been trying for ten years and all of a sudden, God decides to bless us when we least expect it. Oh, Brenda, I *need* a job," she cried.

"You're staying here? Oh, Wyatt, that's the best news I've had in months!" Brenda forced herself in between the close couple on the couch and threw her arms around them both. "We're going to have a baby!" She jumped from the couch and began skipping through the living room. She turned when she realized what this meant. "Of course, you'll live here. I won't take no for an answer."

"Brenda, you may not want to offer us that when we tell you what we did." Barry looked at his wife, "Go ahead, Wyatt. Tell her what *we* did. You've kept it to yourself long enough."

"This really isn't a good time, honey." Wyatt patted her husband's knee, but he remained unfazed by her gesture.

"Wyatt!"

"Okay, okay. When Barry and Luke went to Connecticut, I had them visit your brother," she blurted, turning away from Brenda's gaze.

"My brother? Doug? They saw Doug?" Brenda was baffled.

"We didn't know you two were estranged and we thought it would be a nice surprise to have him call you."

Brenda sat slowly. "I haven't seen him for more than nine years." She tried to comprehend what this meant. Possibly this was the reason for Luke's sudden outburst at the open house. "Did Doug tell you?" Brenda closed her eyes in despair.

"No," Barry answered. "And we didn't ask. He just said you weren't on speaking terms. He also mentioned that Kaitlyn is thirteen now and has two younger brothers, nine and eight."

"I have nephews?" Her voice cracked. Brenda walked numbly into her floral bedroom and dropped onto the rich, cherry pedestal bed. *My sins have finally caught up with me. Forgiven. Maybe by God, but never by my family and now Luke too*. She focused intently on the ceiling fan before finally falling asleep.

fifteen

Luke didn't know what to say to Brenda after the open house. He wanted to tell her was that he was falling in love with her, that his thoughts were filled with spending his days in the *perfect* home in Menlo Park with her. Instead he'd panicked over the many changes taking place in his life and let down the one person he cared about most. Why couldn't he have lost his temper with Olgilvy or the university's housing office? Why did it have to be Brenda?

Luke was shamed by his behavior and too embarrassed to go to her and tell her his feelings. He wallowed in his work, taking on more new patients and more surgeries at the same time. Two weeks passed and he still hadn't called. The longer the time that passed, the worse he felt about calling her.

❧

Star Digital would be public on the stock exchange within the month. Upon hearing she would soon be a multimillionaire, Brenda called Jessie Morgan, the realtor, and inquired about the house she and Luke had visited together.

"Right, you were the attractive couple, very tall. I wouldn't have remembered you, but you two are hard to miss."

"Thank you. I'm calling to find out if you've had any offers."

"It's the oddest thing, but no, we haven't. Such prime real estate too. Are you and your husband interested in making an offer?" the woman asked expectantly. Brenda had hoped that Luke had bought the house, that Miss Morgan would unhappily say it was sold. She hoped that she hadn't heard from him because he'd been so busy with escrow. *This is best,* she thought. *I don't ever want to be the kind of woman who counts on a man for anything. Why would I expect him to buy that house? And even if he had, it wouldn't mean anything to me.* He hadn't made any commitments and by now, it was obvious he wasn't going to. *Not even a phone call.* Brenda shook her head sadly.

"Miss Morgan, you have the wrong impression. I'm not married. My name is Brenda Turner and I'd like to submit an offer. I'll have it to you by tomorrow."

"Who's your agent? I'd be happy to arrange. . ."

"I'm not using a realtor. When can we meet?" Brenda could tell by the extended silence that the realtor was thrown.

"How's ten? My office is. . ."

"Actually, I live in Palo Alto and I'm unable to drive right now. Can you come here?" Brenda's question was pointed and the realtor was quick to agree. The woman took down her address and promised to be there at ten. "My other line is ringing, please feel free to call if something comes up." Brenda buzzed her other line. "Brenda Turner."

"Brenda, it's Luke." Her heart quickened at the unexpected sound of his voice. It had been three long weeks since she'd heard from him and his call sent a flurry of emotions through her, but anger prevailed. "I'm sorry I haven't had a chance to talk with you. It's a long story, but I'm very busy as chief assistant surgeon." Brenda remained stoic as he continued. "I finally had a chance to look at the information sheet on that house. They wanted $700,000 for it," he said incredulously.

"I know," Brenda said as guilt heated her body.

"Buying that house just represents everything I didn't want to become as a doctor. Besides, four bedrooms is far too much for me after my studio. I hope you're not upset I wasted your time." He said apologetically. *Her time, that was all he cared about. He'd wasted her time.* "Brenda, are you still there?"

"I understand the house being too big of a commitment for you." Brenda said solemnly.

"I'm sorry, I've just been feeling so much pressure to pursue things I don't want yet, and I took it out on you. Will you forgive me? I still owe you dinner."

He was feeling pressured to pursue her, so that was it. "Luke, why don't you get settled and call me then?" Brenda wasn't ready to spill the news about her stock option fortune or the perfect house she planned to buy with it. She stared long-ingly into the photograph Wyatt had taken of Luke and Brenda on their first date. His generous smile and laughing eyes, com-bined with his roguish jawline and build sent all her rational thoughts sailing.

"Brenda?"

"Yes, Luke," she said hopefully, hating herself for it.

"I love you. The real me will be back soon." Luke hung up the phone and Brenda stared into the receiver, unsure if she'd dreamt the words or actually heard them. *He loves me? What does he mean? Oh, Luke, I don't care, I love you too.*

❧

Brenda hung up the phone and heard Barry enter the house. His voice was clearly excited and she ran toward the living room.

"I have a job! I start on Monday." Barry's full face widened with a proud grin.

"Barry, already?" Wyatt asked.

"I'm practicing neurology again. I'm going to be assisting Luke with his practice."

"Luke?" Brenda asked, her interest piqued.

"Yes, he's decided to stick it out with the neurosurgery for at least another six months. He's tried to tell Olgilvy about Baylor, but feels this is best for a while. With me, he'll be able to get the surgery experience he wants without abandoning his research patients."

Brenda knew she wouldn't be hearing from Luke anytime soon. Hoping to change the subject, she spilled her news bluntly. "I'm buying a house tomorrow."

"Brenda, you have a house." Wyatt looked stunned.

"I'm buying *another* house in Menlo Park. The Country French house from a few weeks ago. I'm putting an offer on it."

"I don't understand," Wyatt stammered.

"I'll be wealthy beyond my wildest dreams next month, so why not?" Brenda rationalized.

"Because you don't need a house, that's why not. Do you plan to spend everything you've made in the next week?"

"It's an investment, Wyatt. This way, you, Barry, and the baby will have this house and I'll be out of your way. It's completely rent-free until you go back to Africa. My gift to you for all your love and care."

"Brenda, are we bothering you? I thought we'd make a nice threesome. Do you want us to leave?"

Barry, seeing the nature of the discussion, left the two women alone.

"Of course not. The furniture's staying. The new house is French styling, so I'm buying all new furnishings. Light wood, ladder-back chairs, that type of thing. A relaxed, casual elegance. I don't feel well. Please excuse me." Brenda dashed into her room and closed the door, ending any further reprimands. She leaned against the door, listening to Wyatt's quiet footsteps just outside. This was clearly best for everyone. Wyatt and Barry would be alone with their baby and Brenda would just be alone. Again. For the first time, the thought filled her with a cold, empty sensation.

❧

To Brenda's surprise, Luke called every day for two months. He hadn't bought a house, but was renting a small condominium near the hospital. He never visited Brenda nor asked to see her, but he called every evening at nine and asked about her day, her health, and her walk with the Lord. Brenda, against her better judgment, shared everything and wished with all her heart that he was there to hold her. They would talk extensively and when the call ended, Brenda would feel lost, aching for his touch. He finished each conversation by telling her he loved her.

Once a week at church she would see him, but he never acted as more than a casual acquaintance. Occasionally, he would join her, Wyatt, and Barry for lunch after service, but they were never alone. Their phone calls provided the only intimacy in their relationship. Brenda was confused. She had fallen intensely in love with him, but he kept a distance between them that she couldn't cross and she kept her own: She hadn't told him about the house.

She was scheduled to move the following week and she still hadn't mentioned it to Luke. She felt she had betrayed him by buying it and hadn't found the courage to tell him.

Tonight, when he calls, I'll tell him, she vowed. She dressed for her first day back at work, looking at her once-again slender appearance in the mirror.

"Brenda?" Wyatt came to the bedroom door, her rounded belly just beginning to bulge under her loose-fitting T-shirt. Brenda looked at her expectantly. "Barry and I have come up with an amount we'd like to pay you for the house for rent."

Brenda shook her head vehemently. "Absolutely not. Anything you pay me is money that could cure an African child. Besides, it's a write-off for me. Just think of it as the Lord's provision." Brenda waved a hand, dismissing Wyatt and concentrating on her reflection.

"No, Brenda, this is very important to Barry. If you decide to donate the money we pay you, that's your business, but we cannot in good conscience live off you while we're both working. I have no choice. Barry has spoken and he is the leader of our household."

The final words sent an eerie chill through Brenda's spine. Remembering the disturbing acts that her mother had termed Biblical submission, Brenda's respect for Barry swiftly deteriorated and she couldn't hold her tongue. "How can you say that? You've been the breadwinner all summer. Now he suddenly has a job and he's boss?"

"Brenda, it wouldn't matter if I earned *all* the money. It's not like Barry's lazy, he's been gathering missions support." Wyatt's tone was persuasive. "That takes a lot of effort to raise finances and gather medications. Besides, the Bible says the husband is the head of the household."

"My mother always threw that in my face! Every time my father belittled her in front of her friends, or screamed at her for buying a roast that was too expensive, I heard those ridiculous words, 'The husband is the head of the household.' My mother would meekly apologize to her friends for *her* insubordinate behavior then slink back to the store and return the meat that was thirty cents over budget! I'll *never* let that happen! No man will ever tell me how to run *my* life. Just because I'm a Christian doesn't give a man the right to walk all over me!"

"Brenda, there's a lot in the Bible that's hard for a new believer to understand. But everything there has a purpose and God placed it there for good reason." Wyatt spoke softly and sat down beside Brenda at the foot of the bed. Brenda kept her back stiffened, unwilling to bend on the subject. "I want you to read that passage tonight in Ephesians five. There is far more responsibility placed on the husband. I think when you see God's intentions for the husband to care for his wife as Christ cares for the church, you'll see it differently."

"*This* is the very reason I haven't spoken to my family in years."

Wyatt looked intrigued and continued prodding. "I don't mean to disparage your father, especially when he's not here to defend himself, but Brenda, his way worked for your mother. She quietly submitted to his leadership. Possibly, you considered it too harsh, but your mother was happy. Wasn't she?"

"She pretended to be happy, but I heard her quiet sobs when Dad left for work. I saw her mortification when she was left to entertain friends after my father had cut her to shreds for wasting precious coffee on 'a bunch of freeloading gossips.' She may have loved my father, but she wasn't happy."

"You've got to allow God to take that burden from you, Brenda. Hanging on to that anger, not leaving it at the altar for Christ to carry, that's sin." Wyatt surrounded her with loving arms. "Tell me what caused the terrible rift in your family. I think you'll feel better if you do."

Brenda longed to lift the heavy burden from her soul, to share it with Wyatt and allow God to take it away, but she couldn't part with it. She sat gazing into Wyatt's understanding green eyes, wondering if she could let go, knowing she couldn't. *Not yet.*

&

Brenda returned to work happily after her two-month hiatus. Entering her familiar office brought tears to her eyes. Katie was there to greet her with flowers and a balloon bouquet. "Welcome back!" Katie's sweet brown eyes sparkled with her smile. "I left a Balance bar and a mocha on your desk."

Brenda came forward and hugged her assistant fiercely. "I've missed you so much!"

"I'm sorry I haven't seen much of you. We've been so busy with Daydan's birth mother and her visitation rights, I just haven't had the energy."

"Please, Katie, don't worry about me. I'm sorry things are still rocky with Tasha's visitations. I'm praying."

"We appreciate that. God's will be done," Katie said coldly, unable to muster any true feelings of warmth. "Try as I might, I can't resent Tasha for wanting the same thing I do. I just keep hoping that God has a plan that will work for all of us. How are you feeling?"

"Great, I'm off the steroids and back to running. I bought a treadmill and put it right under the air-conditioning vent. It's like running in a cold arctic snow!" Brenda laughed. "The only medication I'm on is Interferon B. I give myself a shot every other day, and I feel almost normal. Just a little dizzy when I'm tired or hot."

"Have you heard from my cousin?" Katie smiled with mock innocence.

"I hear from him every night, but that's as far as it goes, just a nice, solid friendship," Brenda said casually. She sat down proudly at her huge mahogany desk, running her arms across it. "I missed this place."

"I bet." Katie held a pad of paper and rattled off statistics for Brenda's schedule.

"Great. Thanks, Katie. For holding down the fort."

"That's my job. By the way, the stock just hit ninety dollars a share." Katie smiled brilliantly and exited.

Brenda leaped from her desk and kicked her heels together. It had happened, she was now worth nearly four million dollars, including real estate. How she wished her mother and father could see her now. Would they be proud? Or would they still say poor Brenda just couldn't find a man?

Brenda returned home just before nine. She had so much to catch up on at work and her fatigued body couldn't gather the energy to run her treadmill. She could barely manage eating the dinner Wyatt had prepared. The phone rung at precisely nine o'clock and Brenda warmed to Luke's rich voice.

"Hi, sweetheart. How'd things go today?" Luke asked.

"Great, I think I sold the engineering department on my application ideas for the next wave of digital television. On-demand television is closer than ever."

"I can't wait," Luke joked. "What else is happening?"

"That involves a little confession."

"To me?" Luke questioned.

"Kind of. I haven't been fully honest about my recent activities. I bought the Menlo Park house. The one we looked at together." She waited, hoping for a positive answer.

Luke sat down on his kitchen stool, unprepared for the news. "You mean you put an offer down?"

"No, I mean I move in on Saturday. Don't blame Wyatt or Barry, I swore them to secrecy."

Luke looked down at the sparkling engagement ring in the small black box he held. The woman he loved had deceived him and for the life of him, he couldn't understand why she would allow this to go unmentioned. "I don't understand, Brenda. Didn't you think I'd be happy for you?"

"I didn't want you talking me out of it. I wanted the house and paid for it with my own money so it didn't concern you. I had air-conditioning installed and I'm thinking of putting in a pool. There are no stairs—it's completely conducive to MS life."

Luke remained quiet. Brenda was planning a life alone, a life that didn't include him. It was clear she was capable of life without him. That's why he was so attracted to her in the first place. He dropped the ring box dejectedly onto the counter.

Go to her.

God's words were clear, and before he had a chance to think, he asked impatiently, "Are you available for dinner Saturday?"

She waited a moment before speaking, "I—uh. . .guess so. So what about the house?"

"What about it? Are you available Saturday or not?" he asked curtly.

"Yes," she said simply.

"Be ready at six. Dress nicely. I'll see you then."

"Wait a minute. Do you remember how to get to the house?" Brenda inquired.

"I'll pick you up in Palo Alto." Luke hung up the phone, thoroughly annoyed about Brenda's recent moves. *She's so blasted independent, but what good would it do her to live a wealthy, lonely life?* Moving away from Wyatt and Barry certainly wasn't a step in the right direction and Luke was determined to set Brenda on the straight and narrow. Brenda had done everything in her adult lifetime alone and Luke was determined to show her that two are better than one.

sixteen

After working all week, by Friday night Brenda could feel her body giving in to the disease. Her double vision returned slightly and her left leg tingled with numbness. She had exceeded her limits at work, coming home each night later and later, sometimes even missing Luke's nine o'clock phone call. She fell into bed ready to celebrate the weekend and awaited Luke's call, which was punctual.

"Evenin', gorgeous." Luke's voice filled her senses.

"Hi Luke."

"Are you ready for the big move?" It was the first time he'd mentioned the new house and Brenda rejoiced at the possibility that he was happy for her.

"Not really. I'm afraid I overdid it this week. The movers can handle it. I don't have much, just my office and a sofa or two. I'll just rest at the new house and oversee everything."

"I had a feeling your job might continue to be an issue." Luke's voice was even, not showing the slightest hint of judgment. "Maybe God has something better for you," he said cryptically.

"It seems I'm stuck. I had always planned my own business, but I'd never get independent health insurance now. And who's going to hire me with MS? Even if it's in remission, I'd still have to disclose it on an application. With my meds costing nearly a thousand a month, I'm afraid I'm unhirable. Even with my excellent track record, I'm not worth the risk."

"Stop worrying. God has the answer," Luke said.

"I know, but I hope He speaks soon, these hours are killing me and I don't ever want to be sick like that again. Not ever. I'll sell this house first and live off the proceeds. God has given me the financial ability to quit, I just don't have an answer to the health insurance problem. He will provide, though. I know

He will." Brenda's voice was determined.

"Absolutely, He will. I love you, Brenda, and can't wait to see you tomorrow." Luke knew how God would provide. Brenda would have Luke's health insurance as soon as she was his wife, and marrying a neurologist would most certainly be a benefit. She wouldn't have to work another day if she chose not to. Luke's plan was coming together nicely.

"I love you too, Luke," Brenda was finally able to say the words and she felt immense relief at releasing her true feelings.

❧

Luke arrived Saturday evening wearing a new pair of espresso brown slacks with a classic matching houndstooth check sport coat, "Luke Marcusson, I do believe you spent some money!" Brenda allowed Luke into the house and circled the doctor, investigating his new suit.

"Very funny. You look stunning as usual," Luke replied, kissing her gently on her high cheekbone. She felt his touch pulse through her body. Brenda was wearing a dress she'd had custom designed for a work event. It was a muted aqua blue that matched her eyes, covered by tastefully placed beaded sparkles. The v-neck was cut deeper than normal for her, but a well-placed chiffon wrap preserved her modesty. Her hair was pulled up into a loose bun, with soft blond ringlets framing her face.

"Thank you," she said shyly. "Where are we going?"

"Somewhere I hope we'll never forget," he said mysteriously. "Where's Wyatt and Barry?"

"They spent the day away to allow the movers access. I guess they went out to dinner. I haven't had much rest. I hope I'll be good company tonight."

"You're always good company." Luke offered his arm and led Brenda to his sporty, yet practical new car. They drove for nearly twenty minutes before stopping at a large gate surrounded by foliage on a remote roadside speckled with bicyclists. Luke got out of the car and unlocked the gates, drove in and locked them behind him. Inside was a small, abandoned parking lot surrounded by large trees with a small dirt pathway between.

"Luke, where are we?"

"You'll see. Just be patient."

Luke assisted Brenda out of the car and opened the trunk, pulling out a huge wicker basket. They walked along the path and soon the sound of rushing water invaded the stillness. The path soon opened to a clearing where a huge, white circular columned structure loomed above them. It was surrounded by a perimeter of small marble steps leading to a great pool below, which was enveloped in a sea of grass.

"Luke, it's so beautiful. What is this place?"

"It's the Pulgas Water Temple. This is where the water from the Hetch Hetchy River near Yosemite enters the Crystal Springs Reservoir."

"It's perfect." Brenda ran up the marble steps and marveled at the rush of crystal clear water running through it. She pulled the clip from her hair and let her long, lustrous golden curls fall to her back. "I feel like a princess here."

"As it should be." Luke kept his eyes fastened on Brenda, delighting in her every movement as she skipped across the idyllic scene.

"Where is everybody? I would think people would flock here."

"It's closed most of the time. Vandals and drag racers on the road outside keep it off limits. I have a friend who works for the water department. He gave me access. Are you hungry?"

"We're eating here?" Brenda's blue eyes brightened.

"Yes, I've packed dinner. I even shopped at the natural foods store. There's nothing on our menu with anything that violates the MS diet. No easy task, I might add."

"It's a pain, isn't it? And how I miss a good piece of prime rib."

"Not when I tell you our menu." Luke took her hand and climbed down the steps. Once on the grass near the shallow, elongated pool, he produced a red and white checked table cloth, snapping it smartly and laying it smoothly on the ground with a theatrical flair. On top of it he laid two matching chair cushions and set the "table" with real white china. He helped her to her seat and spread the feast before her. "First, we start with a fine appetizer; spinach-stuffed mushrooms, handmade by Wyatt. Next we have our main course, lobster salad, followed by Raspberry Bavarian, courtesy of Dr. Swank's MS-approved recipes. Of course, we'll wash it down with a fine vintage." Luke lifted a bottle over his forearm and spoke in his best French accent, "Chateau du sparkling apple juice." Taking out two champagne flutes, he filled them.

"I don't know what to say, I'm so flattered." She looked at his warm hazel eyes and knew she didn't want to say anything. She wanted to show him, to feel the fire of his kiss and be beside him under the dwindling sunlight, amid the soothing sounds of flowing water. Luke lit a candle and she shook the tempting thought from her head.

They ate without a word, searching one another's eyes and basking in their ever-growing love for one another. When they finished the meal, Luke hurriedly threw the dishes into the basket and came close. He lifted her into the canopy of the water temple and she squealed in surprise.

He placed her next to the well of rushing water and bent down on one knee. "Brenda Turner, I have waited so long for this day. I have stayed away for fear my physical attraction would prove too strong for us to bear. My heart's desire was to know you intimately, but I couldn't trust myself with you alone. That's why I've relied on the telephone so that I might learn everything about you without letting us both down."

Brenda was overcome by her own emotions, and happy tears filled her eyes at the revelation that he had stayed away so that he might pursue their relationship. The slight hint of green in his brown eyes mesmerized her and she willed herself to allow him to continue talking, when she really wanted to bend down and make full use of his lips.

"I've watched you grow so deeply into your faith, becoming a woman of God that I know He delights in. I've watched you battle your disease with grace and dignity, and I know, Brenda, that my life will never be the same without you and I don't want it to be. Brenda Turner, will you marry me?" He held up the most magnificent ring she'd ever seen. It was a bright blue, brilliant-cut sapphire, encompassed between two smaller brilliant-cut diamonds and held up by a classic platinum band. It was obviously an estate piece; jewelers didn't make rings like that anymore.

Marriage? Brenda was stunned speechless, her blue eyes wide in shock. *Of course, a man like Luke would want to be married, but how can I say yes?* How could she when she'd watched her mother and her years of toil and pain? How could she, knowing she might not be healthy or able to care for his children? How could she when she already had everything she'd planned?

Brenda cringed. She was most afraid of Luke's careful spending habits. She had worked hard for her money and she couldn't bear to hand control to a man. Not even an upright, godly man like Luke. She closed her eyes momentarily. Opening them, she looked into his expectant gaze and knew her lips would deceive her and reply yes. So she turned away, looking down at the rushing water beside her.

"I can't marry you, Luke. I'm sorry." She couldn't offer more, even at the risk of his feelings. If she did, she would certainly betray her true feelings. *Why couldn't we have continued the way we were? Why did you have to ruin it with a marriage proposal?*

Luke stood slowly and closed the ring box over the exquisite sapphire. "I see." Brenda had never heard a cold chill in his voice before. It was tempered and carefully restrained. He straightened to his full six-foot-three stature and squared his broad shoulders. "That ends the entertainment portion of our evening." Luke held his arm out but Brenda just couldn't bring herself to grasp it. His touch would break her resolve. She walked swiftly to the car, waiting at the passenger door while he collected the picnic basket.

Brenda wanted to make things right, but words failed her. She could think of nothing that might offer an acceptable excuse to Luke. How could she tell him that she had always dreamed of true love, but that had never included marriage? The fantasy always stopped before the altar. The silence in the car lasted for a painful eternity. Brenda's only request was that Luke take her to the Palo Alto house, because the Menlo Park home would only be salt in the wound to her beloved. She couldn't endure a night in an empty, lonely house tonight. Luke dropped her at the door and she scurried into the house, bidding him a quick, obligatory good night.

Brenda ran to her bedroom and threw herself on the bed, her whole frame quaking from her deafening sobs. She cried for over an hour before she heard the front door open. Brenda hurriedly sat up, wiping the tears from her cheeks and hugging her long legs to her chest.

"Brenda, we're home!" Wyatt announced shortly before appearing in the doorway. "Oh, you are here. I thought you might be at the new. . .what's the matter? You look a terrible sight."

"Luke asked me to marry him."

"Brenda, that's wonderful! Why are you crying?" Wyatt went to the bedroom door. "Barry, I'll be a minute." She closed the door and sat at the edge of Brenda's bed. "You said yes, right?"

"No." Brenda inhaled roughly, choking over her cries. She carried on for several minutes before looking Wyatt in the eyes. "It's not something you'd understand. I'm just not the marrying kind. I'm not like you or my mother."

"No, you're not, but I don't understand what that has to do with marrying the man you love. Let go of this before you lose the man I know you love! You owe me an explanation and I'm not leaving until I get it!" Wyatt crossed her arms defiantly.

Brenda saw fire in Wyatt's green eyes, a wrathful intensity she'd never seen in her gentle friend. Brenda began slowly, "I don't know where to start." Seeing that Wyatt's demeanor hadn't changed, she went on, "My parents were strong believers in the Bible. They went to a strict, frightening church where I never saw an ounce of love portrayed. Their view of God was that He was vengeful and terrifying; He was never tempered with love, and I guess you could say that was how our home life was as well."

"Go on," Wyatt stated impatiently.

"My mother felt a woman's *only* calling in life was to get married and have children. They saved every extra cent to send my brother to college, but I wouldn't *need* college. When I didn't have a husband after high school, they finally relented and said they'd pay for community college. You can probably guess the rest; I didn't find a husband there either. Probably because that's the last thing I ever wanted."

"What about your brother?"

"Doug was raised to believe the man was the head of the household. My mom and dad were determined to see their pattern continue in our lives. I would be the submissive housewife and my brother the strong husband. Unfortunately, they did everything for Doug while they left me to my own devices. They figured I wouldn't need their help because a husband would soon manage everything for me. I learned to do everything for myself while Doug was left virtually reliant upon them. I earned a full scholarship and finished my MBA at Stanford Business School. Doug never did finish, he didn't have the least idea of how to manage for himself. Last I heard, he was a stay-at-home dad and his wife works to provide for them. He was happy with the arrangement and I don't fault him, but still it's ironic."

"That still doesn't explain why you're not speaking."

"My parents died of carbon monoxide poisoning while I was at Stanford. My dad was too cheap to replace the old furnace. It was during finals week and I couldn't risk losing my scholarship to go back east. My entire family was mortified at my career goals, that they would take precedence over my parent's funeral. They all thought I was so driven because no man would have me. My grandparents had arranged for me to meet a carefully selected man from their church. Going back, even for the funeral, felt like death to me. I didn't want to lose my freedom again. And I still don't."

"You can't possibly think Luke cares about your money." Wyatt's eyes had tears in them now.

"I know how carefully he spends it and I won't stand for somebody telling me I can't buy boneless chicken because it's cheaper to debone it myself."

Wyatt began laughing and covered her mouth, trying to stop. "You're not going to marry the man you love because you think he might make you debone a chicken?"

Brenda also began giggling through her tears. "No, I'm not going to marry him because I love him more than anything on this earth. How could I ever say no to him? If he told me to buy the whole darn chicken and pluck it myself, I just might do it." The two broke into laughter again.

Wyatt soon became serious again. "Luke is not like your father. He relishes your independence."

"No, but he would be the head of the household, right?" Brenda asked sheepishly.

"That's what the Bible says, but Brenda, God's plan is for you to submit to Luke's will because he would act in the best interest of his family. The full responsibility of his household rests upon him. That's a huge sacrifice for a man to make."

"I don't want to submit to Luke." Brenda admitted stubbornly.

"You don't want to submit to God either. I know all this is new to you, but you've got to learn to trust in God and not your wealth. Money and material goods will all pass away. When Christ returns do you want to be left with your stuff or lifted into the clouds with Jesus?" Wyatt patted her arm and left. Before closing the door behind her, she left her with one last thought. "Read the story of the rich young ruler in Matthew 19. God is giving you all His blessings, including a man after His own heart. Which will you choose? You'll never truly own anything unless you give it to God first."

seventeen

Brenda continued to read her Bible and pray, but skipped over any passages that spoke of money. *God doesn't live on earth, He doesn't understand the importance of a healthy bank account here in Silicon Valley. The Bible was written a long time ago, certainly some things have changed.* Her financial portfolio was her compensation for this terrible disease she endured.

Luke no longer called and Brenda only saw him occasionally at church. He never sat with her, spoke with her, or mentioned anything of his proposal. If pressed with unavoidable contact, he would simply nod and be on his way or ask rigidly about her health.

Brenda ached at his coldness. She longed to rush to him, but Luke never allowed her the opportunity. Worst of all was the knowledge that she loved him, and that she lived in *their* perfect home—alone. Brenda didn't feel the completeness in the Menlo Park house that she'd felt when buying the Victorian. As a matter of fact, she didn't feel anything about the big, sterile country home that once seemed as warm as a cold winter night in front of a roaring fire.

Only her time alone with God filled her with warmth. God had been faithful to honor Brenda's prayers of physical healing, but her soul still ached for something more she couldn't describe.

As winter neared, Brenda's discontentment grew and her ability to keep up with the pressures of her job as vice president dwindled. After deep prayer, Brenda knew she would have to resign her executive post. One overcast October morning, she humbly entered the office of her general manager and asked for a smaller assignment. Knowing she wouldn't be able to handle the tasks of a similar position elsewhere, and in desperate need of health coverage, Brenda asked to be a marketing manager within her own department.

The first week of November, Brenda bid farewell to her spacious corner office overlooking the man-made lakes on the company campus, and moved into a simple, gray cubicle. Her new boss and former rival, Mike Wilcox, took over her old mahogany desk and sweeping water views.

Brenda had moved the last few boxes into her cubicle when Katie appeared. "I got Mike's old cubicle. It's the biggest one there is," Brenda said enthusiastically, while she fought back tears. Katie came forward and hugged her. "I won't have anybody to get me a mocha or a Balance bar."

"I'll still do that as long as I'm here. I did that because I was your friend, Brenda, not your slave. In case you haven't heard, secretaries don't do those things anymore. We're administrative assistants now. You're supposed to get your own coffee."

Brenda broke into laughter.

"Seriously, you were a great boss. Who else would have gotten me such a huge share of stock? I'm nearly as rich as any of the managers in this place."

"Well, you did more work than most of them did," Brenda stated truthfully.

Katie pulled forward a chair and motioned for Brenda to sit. "Jacob and I talked to an architect last night."

"An architect?"

"We're adding on to the East Palo Alto house. We've gotten to know Tasha pretty well since she's been visiting Daydan and we found out she dreams of being a nurse like Wyatt."

"I thought Tasha was getting custody of Daydan."

"She will have custody, but it seems we're getting custody of Tasha. She's going to live with us. We just agreed two nights ago. Thanks to you and our stock money, we can afford to build a new private room and pay for Tasha's college. I'm quitting my job, so I can be home with Daydan during the day while she attends school. Day's grandmother is getting too feeble to keep up with him all day long. He's got more energy than a speeding train. We've grown to love Tasha so much and being around us, she's seen how much we love Day and it's made a huge difference. I don't think she wants him to lose that, especially with Jacob for a father."

"You're leaving?" Brenda was stunned, unable to fathom life at work without her Christian sister. Life appeared bleaker than ever. She was alone in her big empty house and now she would be alone at work as well.

"Brenda, I'm only in East Palo Alto and if you're afraid to come see us, we'll come see you. We'll see you every Sunday at church, like we always do."

"It's just not the same. It was so much easier to come to work, knowing you'd be here if I had an attack or needed support. I always thought I'd have financial freedom to leave, but now that I have the money, I'm stuck because of health benefits."

"Keep praying, Brenda, and stop putting your trust in money and start looking to Him." Katie looked upward.

❧

Luke had learned all he cared to about computer-aided surgery. He was yearning to get back to his first love of neurology and his patients. Barry and Wyatt had almost raised the needed support to get back to Africa and they would be leaving within months after the new baby arrived. It was time to confront Dr. Olgilvy. Luke had prayed for a way out, but God had remained silent on the subject and his deadline grew ever nearer.

LeAnne, Luke's nurse, appeared in the doorway to his office. "Barry called. Wyatt just had an eight-pound, seven-ounce girl and they've named her Grace. They're over at the hospital. Barry won't be in today, so your first appointment is at ten."

Luke ran to the hospital, anxious to see Barry's first child. He was breathless when he arrived.

Wyatt looked exhausted, but glowing. She held the baby girl in her arms and her euphoria was apparent. Barry hovered behind her, with a new father's pride. "Have you ever seen a more beautiful sight?" she asked, noticing Luke.

"No. A beautiful baby in your arms is probably the most precious sight God will ever grant me. I'm so happy for you both." Luke bent down and kissed Wyatt's forehead.

"We've waited so long for this and it's better than I ever dreamed it would be. I feel more love for this child than I could ever put into words." Tears streamed down Wyatt's cheeks while she wore her widest smile.

"Wyatt, she's beautiful. Just like her mother." Brenda appeared by the bed with an extravagant bouquet of flowers and a huge teddy bear with a big pink collar. Under her arm, she carried a box wrapped in pink ribbons and bows, with a sterling silver rattle as a centerpiece of the wrap.

"How did you know it was a girl?" Barry asked, noting the pink.

"I didn't. I have the exact bounty at home in blue, in case it was a boy." They all laughed and watched the baby intensely. "May I hold her, Wyatt?" Brenda meekly asked.

"Oh, please do," Wyatt answered. Brenda sat in a nearby chair to avoid any unexpected dizziness and took the precious bundle from Barry. Tears filled her eyes and Luke was torn by the scene, wishing he didn't have to watch the woman he loved cradle a baby. *She might have been ours, Lord.* Brenda inadvertently looked at him and the storm of emotion was too great.

"I've got to get back to the office. My partner's nowhere to be found today and I've got a full load of his patients." Luke patted Barry on the back and kissed Wyatt's cheek. Luke exited as quickly as he could without a glance or remark toward Brenda.

❧

Brenda spent the entire morning with tiny Grace, until the newborn cried for her mother. As she suckled, Barry left the women alone. "I'll go check on a few patients, while I'm here," he offered, by way of excuse.

"Luke looks great, doesn't he?" Wyatt asked.

Brenda nodded. "My new job is going well, but by Friday night, I'm worn to the bone." Brenda's robotic conversation did not go unnoticed by her closest friend.

"You know we'll be leaving for Africa soon. I thought you might want to place an ad for the Victorian. We won't be needing it after the first of the year."

"I'll get that done. Thanks," she said absently.

"Why are you doing this to yourself? You love Luke, I know you love Luke. Brenda, tell him before he moves on with his life." Even with her strength depleted from childbirth, Wyatt remained steadfast in spurring Brenda.

"It's not that easy, Wyatt. Luke and I have different outlooks on the future. It's just like the reason he said you two broke up; our lives are going in different directions."

"Do you think I wanted to abandon the cushy life of a Stanford doctor's wife to go live in a desert across the world, with critters I'd never heard of, and bugs the size of compact cars?"

"You're a nurse, Wyatt. You love people."

"I love people, but not enough to forfeit a fancy lifestyle for them. Only God could change my heart—and He did. Now I *want* my daughter raised in Africa and I want to grow old, seeing thousands saved by the medical help we can provide. But none of it is from me. *I* could have cared less. Without God's prodding I would have never known that world existed. God restored your health, Brenda, now ask yourself what you'll do with that gift."

"Everyone's leaving me. You and Barry, Katie and Jacob. I've lost you all in the blink of an eye." Tears of self-pity overcame her, but Wyatt was without sympathy.

"You haven't lost everyone. God is still here and He's left you a man who loves you deeply. Did you see Luke's eyes when he watched you with Grace? For cryin' out loud, Brenda, go tell him you love him before it's too late. Is any amount of money really worth his feelings? Did you read about the rich young ruler yet?"

"I read it. A rich young man asked Jesus what he needed to do to gain eternal life. Jesus told him first not to murder, nor commit adultery, not to steal, nor to give false testimony, and to honor his mother and father, and love his neighbor as himself. Then he needed to go and sell everything he had."

"Why? Jesus said all we have to do is place our faith in Him, so why would He tell him that?" Wyatt persisted.

"Because he'd have no use for it. But we live in an expensive area, Wyatt. Obviously, I can't go sell everything I own."

"Jesus told the young man to go sell everything he had because the young man's sin was covetousness and his riches were between God and him, keeping him from a true relationship. There's nothing wrong with having money, unless the money has you."

"But the Bible says he went away sad because he had great wealth, so maybe he did give it up! And he was sad because he had so much, that makes sense. If Jesus asked me to sell my houses or stocks, I would."

"The young man turned his back on Jesus! If he truly were going to follow Jesus, he would have left with joy and not thought twice about his things. He didn't sell them and I don't think you'd sell yours either, Brenda."

"Are you saying I'm not saved? What about all that saved by grace business?"

"Brenda, you are saved. You've been washed clean by Christ, but you're holding back your possessions from Him, unable to take full advantage of what He offers. God doesn't need your things, Brenda. I'm just saying, until you offer them, you'll never own true freedom."

"Take care of Grace. I'll be back tomorrow. I love you, Wyatt, even though you're a nag," she added quietly. She smiled and kissed her friend's cheek and the baby once more.

"I love you, Brenda. I'll always be there for you."

❦

Brenda walked into the hospital corridor and exhaled deeply. Wyatt was right, Brenda no longer received pleasure from her things. They were a constant reminder of what she didn't have: Luke, Katie, and soon Wyatt and Barry. God was slowly taking her loved ones away one by one, making her new home feel sparser and emptier with each passing moment.

"Miss Turner?" Brenda turned to see a handsome, middle-aged doctor approaching.

"Dr. Olgilvy, what a nice surprise. How are you?" Brenda took his offered hand and shook it sincerely.

"It's Frederick, and I'm fine. Are you here to have lunch with Luke?"

"No, I'm visiting a friend who just had a baby, actually—the prettiest baby ever," Brenda bragged like a proud grandmother.

"The best reason to come to the hospital," Dr. Olgilvy commented.

"No kidding. After those MS corticosteroid treatments, I didn't think I'd ever step into a hospital by choice again." Brenda realized suddenly that Dr. Olgilvy didn't know about her disease and she felt like kicking herself.

"Brenda, you have MS?" Dr. Olgilvy asked incredulously.

"Yes, I thought Luke might have told you. That's actually how we met. He was my doctor until we began seeing each other on a personal level." Just being able to say his name freely felt like a victory.

"Have you had lunch yet?" he asked.

"No, actually, I haven't." Brenda could feel her stomach grumbling.

"Gloria's waiting in my office; why don't you join us for lunch?"

Brenda wanted to say no, but how could she? Luke's boss was a man of prominent stature and more importantly, a man who had power over his career. It was the least she could do for Luke, after she had so blatantly disregarded his feelings.

Entering Dr. Olgilvy's office, Brenda noticed a petite brunette chatting easily with Mrs. Olgilvy. She wore a pale pink nurse's uniform and it was cut tightly to show off her slender young body.

"Brenda, what a nice surprise. This is Nurse Eve Moore. Have you two met?" Gloria asked. "Eve, this is Brenda Turner, Luke's girlfriend."

The pretty nurse came toward Brenda, extending a hand and producing a counterfeit smile. "So, Luke's into blonds now." The nurse looked Brenda up and down, eyeing her jealously. "Tsk, tsk, such a fickle thing he is." Brenda filled with rage and she clenched her jaw tightly, at a loss to respond kindly. *How dare this impudent little nurse disparage Luke in front of the*

Olgilvys. Sensing her anger, Eve continued, "Luke and I go way back. Hasn't he mentioned me? No? Isn't that just like Luke." She looked back at the Olgilvys, seeing if they were interested in her comments.

"A doctor that looks like Luke is bound to have a history," Gloria offered, by way of a white flag, hoping to dispel the obvious clash between the two women.

Brenda decided to put an end to the awful scene quickly. "Shall we go?" Brenda asked cheerfully, while looking down over Eve Moore's small frame.

The Olgilvys eagerly agreed and they spent a delightful lunch discussing Brenda's favorite topic: Luke Marcusson. She learned so much about Luke's new surgical skills and she was further impressed by each sentence. She had no idea the technique or abilities required to perform his latest job as assistant chief to Dr. Olgilvy.

The Olgilvys continued to talk of their latest stock deals and art purchases. Hearing them rattle off prices and money gains, Brenda heard the characteristics in herself that she hated most and wondered if God was trying to tell her something.

❧

After lunch, Brenda ran back into Wyatt's hospital room. "Wyatt! Wyatt!" she whispered loudly, rousing the young mother from her sleep. "Please wake up."

"Brenda, is everything okay?" Wyatt wiped her eyes with the back of her hand.

"Is the baby okay?" she asked with a look of alarm.

"Everybody's fine!"

"Brenda, what. . ."

"You were right. Money hasn't helped me, it only stirs up my worst attributes. My father loved me, I didn't realize that until now. He would never have been impressed with my accomplishments, because they are all based on earthly things! He wanted me to know God, a husband was secondary! I allowed my father to go without ever telling him I loved him. Now I'll have to wait, but I can't do that to Luke. I've got to tell him how I feel! I've been living on faith in my money, not

God. I allowed myself to believe in God because I knew *I* could take care of everything! That's what you've been trying to tell me, isn't it?"

"Yes, Brenda," Wyatt said through tears.

"After we talked about the rich young ruler, God gave me a prime example in the Olgilvys. They have everything I thought I wanted, but their lives are so empty. Did you know they never had children because they'd interfere with her tennis game? After seeing Grace, I knew what I really wanted. I just pray I'm not too late. When I get home, I'm signing my stock over to your ministry. It's worth about three million dollars right now. If I'm going to trust in God, I need to trust Him fully."

"How—?" Wyatt was wide-eyed.

"I just heard two very wealthy people who sounded very poor in soul to me," Brenda said. "I need to do this."

"What about Luke? What changed your mind about him?"

"That was just simple, unbridled jealously. I heard this nurse talking about him like he was a piece of meat and I knew immediately that I don't want him in anyone's arms but mine! I gotta go. Love you!" Brenda ran out the door in her excitement and straight across the street to Luke's office.

Wyatt looked up to the ceiling and mouthed, "Thank You."

eighteen

Brenda rushed into Luke's office and was met in her breathless state by Luke's unfriendly nurse. "Can I help you?" she asked icily.

"LeAnne, I need to see Luke. Will you please tell him I'm waiting? I know we've had our differences in the past, but please, this is very important."

"He's in his office. Go ahead," she said, with a hint of a smile.

Brenda raced into his office before her resolve left her. She closed the door behind her and Luke looked up from his chair, confused. "Brenda, are you all right?" He stood to his full stature and Brenda thought she'd melt at the sight of him.

"Never better. Would you mind sitting?" she asked shyly and he obediently sat back down. "I had lunch with the Olgilvys today. They think very highly of you." Brenda tried to catch her breath, but her chest pumped wildly.

"Did you come all the way over here to tell me that?" Luke asked briskly.

"No." Brenda walked toward him, keeping her eyes firmly directed at his. As she approached, he rolled his chair back away from the desk. Brenda sat suddenly and uninvited in his lap, and gazed intently into his captivating hazel eyes. Stroking his rugged jawline gently with her long fingers, she began her unrehearsed speech.

"Luke, I know I can be hardheaded and exasperating, but worst of all, I can be extremely foolish. I thought we could continue without marriage, that I wouldn't become ensnared in what my parents planned for me. I know now that my father wasn't the best role model, but I also know that he did what he thought was best. What I'm trying to say is that I trust you, Luke. I trust you to do what's best for me. Just like the day you kidnapped me and dragged me back to the hospital. You brought me back my eyesight, and more importantly, you showed me that sometimes you do know what's best for me, more so than I do."

"What is it you want, Brenda? My forgiveness? Consider it granted," he said coolly.

Brenda took his face in her hands and came mere inches from him. She could feel his warm breath and her own rapidly beating heart. She whispered softly. "No, Luke, I want you completely as my husband and my lover and the head of my household." Tears overcame her.

"Brenda Turner, you are exasperating!" He stood up to leave, but moved her into the chair.

"Luke, I'm sorry. I didn't. . ."

"Just be quiet for five minutes, will you, please?"

Brenda crossed her arms in her lap and Luke returned and knelt down beside her. "I am head of the household. I do the asking. Understood?"

"Yes, sir!" She saluted.

He stood and began to walk out of the office once again. "Luke, that's just cruel. If you just wanted to play with my heart. . ."

"Brenda, what did I just tell you?" He looked back, his warm eyes smiling.

"I'm shutting up." Brenda used her hands to close the pretend zipper over her mouth.

Luke returned moments later and knelt beside her. "Miss Turner, I think you are the most beautiful, exhausting woman I have ever laid eyes upon and I will do you proud as head of your household. Say you'll be my wife." Luke held up the tiny black velvet box with the familiar sapphire sparkling inside it.

"Yes, Luke. YES!" She jumped from the chair and almost bowled him over. He stood awkwardly to his feet and they enveloped each other in a giant hug.

"I'm curious. What changed your mind?" He looked down and kissed the top of her head.

"I'm embarrassed to admit it, but this vixen, Nurse Moore, at the hospital."

"Eve?" Luke was dumbfounded.

"That's her. That conniving little tease implied in front of Dr. and Mrs. Olgilvy that you two had an affair. I knew you had better taste in women, but it sure got me to thinking that I didn't want any better women coming along. The thought of you with someone else was more than I could handle. It was fine when it was you alone, but you with someone else—that did it. Besides, with Wyatt as your ex-girlfriend, I knew you were bound to find some sweet, gentle little thing and then you'd know better than to come back to me."

Luke laughed uproariously. "I doubt that, Brenda. You've got a couple things in your favor. First of all, you're devastatingly beautiful and more importantly, I'm head over heels in love with that opinionated, defiant, hardheaded, godly woman that lives inside. Remind me to send a bouquet of roses to Eve Moore. I owe that woman a great deal."

"Besides, I have one more alternative therapy I can't try without you," Brenda said sheepishly, her cheeks tinged with pink.

"What would that be?"

"Pregnancy. It seems the hormones have some astounding effect on multiple sclerosis that causes remission. So, next bout, we've got a date."

"Let's hope there won't be any further bouts, but that doesn't have to alter our plans." Luke kissed his bride-to-be again and broke himself away reluctantly.

"What were you doing with Olgilvy, anyway?"

"We had lunch with Gloria, of course. By the way, he would understand if you wanted to cut back on surgeries. He wasn't aware of my disease, but now he says he understands why you're so involved in multiple sclerosis issues," Brenda replied innocently.

"I've been trying to accomplish that for six months. How is it you managed to sign my partial resignation in one lunch hour?"

Brenda only shrugged.

"Seriously, Brenda. I owe you and the Ogilvys a big apology. Lying got me into that mess and I'm going to come clean with Olgilvy and explain myself. I've asked God to forgive me and I hope that you will too. That was a terrible example I set, telling others you were my girlfriend before it was true."

"I knew it wasn't typical of you, Luke. I could tell by how uneasy it made you, not to mention what Wyatt and Barry told me about your integrity."

The two locked in a kiss, resolving to leave lying in their past.

epilogue

August 12
Dear Wyatt, Barry, and Grace,

Brenda has been in complete remission for nearly a year now. We're praising the Lord for His provisions and hoping we can claim victory over multiple sclerosis for good. Glad to hear your ministry is thriving. Brenda was delighted to hear that the money has helped to save so many lives already.

I finally relented and bought a "tax shelter" in the form of a business office for Brenda. She has started a new job in East Palo Alto, running a nonprofit program that equips the poor for the workplace. The biggest change in her is seeing the compassion in her heart for these people. I think she started the ministry with a chip on her shoulder, but God showed her the devastation caused by being unable to provide for your family and her heart has changed.

We visited Brenda's brother last month. They had a rough time, but I think things will eventually work out. Brenda promised to visit again and she delighted in her niece and nephews.

The best piece of news I have is that Brenda is pregnant with our first child. Please pray for her and the baby's continued health. As for me, I'm performing between one and two surgeries a week and keeping my practice full. Olgilvy wants to make sure I devote enough time to MS to ensure Brenda's future. Baylor finally called, but I turned them down. God has called me here.

In His Love,
Luke

A Letter To Our Readers

Dear Reader:

In order that we might better contribute to your reading enjoyment, we would appreciate your taking a few minutes to respond to the following questions. When completed, please return to the following:

Rebecca Germany, Managing Editor
Heartsong Presents
PO Box 719
Uhrichsville, Ohio 44683

1. Did you enjoy reading *To Truly See?*
   - ❑ Very much. I would like to see more books by this author!
   - ❑ Moderately
     I would have enjoyed it more if _____

   _____

2. Are you a member of **Heartsong Presents**? ❑Yes ❑No
   If no, where did you purchase this book? _____

   _____

3. What influenced your decision to purchase this book? (Check those that apply.)

❑ Cover	❑ Back cover copy
❑ Title	❑ Friends
❑ Publicity	❑ Other_____

4. How would you rate, on a scale from 1 (poor) to 5 (superior), the cover design? _____

5. On a scale from 1 (poor) to 10 (superior), please rate the following elements.

    ___Heroine   ___Plot

    __ Hero   __Inspirational theme

    __ Setting   __Secondary characters

6. What settings would you like to see covered in **Heartsong Presents** books?_____

_____

_____

7. What are some inspirational themes you would like to see treated in future books?_____

_____

_____

8. Would you be interested in reading other **Heartsong Presents** titles? ❑ Yes   ❑ No

9. Please check your age range:
   ❑ Under 18   ❑ 18-24   ❑ 25-34
   ❑ 35-45   ❑ 46-55   ❑ Over 55

10. How many hours per week do you read? _____

Name _____

Occupation_____

Address_____

City_____ State_____ Zip _____

WHEN I'M ON MY KNEES

Anita Corrine Donihue

Prayers especially for women, prayers that emanate from
the heart, prayers that deal with friendship, family, and
peace. Packaged in a beautifully printed leatherette cover,
women will also find hymns and poems that focus
on prayer in their everyday lives.

About the author:
Anita Corrine Donihue, a teacher with thirty years
of experience, is the coauthor of *Apples for a Teacher*
and *Joy to the World,* two very popular titles
from Barbour Books.

(212 pages, Leatherette, 4" x 6¾")

······Hearts❤ng······

HEARTSONG PRESENTS *TITLES AVAILABLE NOW:*

Presents

Great Inspirational Romance at a Great Price!

Heartsong Presents books are inspirational romances in contemporary and historical settings, designed to give you an enjoyable, spirit-lifting reading experience. You can choose wonderfully written titles from some of today's best authors like Veda Boyd Jones, Yvonne Lehman, Tracie Peterson, Nancy N. Rue, and many others.

When ordering quantities less than twelve, above titles are $2.95 each.
Not all titles may be available at time of order.